Kate

MW01254423

Mrs. McG   rty

by

Larry Dickens

This book is a work of fiction. Places, events, and situations in this story are purely fictional. Any resemblance to actual persons, living or dead, is coincidental.

© 2002 by Larry Dickens. All rights reserved.

No part of this book may be reproduced, restored in a retrieval system, or transmitted by means, electronic, mechanical, photocopying, recording, or otherwise, without written consent from the author.

ISBN: 0-7596-9244-0

This book is printed on acid free paper.

Front cover design by Elaine Gotham, Gotham City Design

Front cover photograph copyright © 1992 John Mueser and Finger Lakes Images

Back cover photograph copyright © 1995 Susan Prislopski

1st Books - rev. 01/22/02

For Hillary and Lindsey

THE RAKE

"It was the worst of times, it was the best of times," Erika Reisling said to herself on occasion. Today it was the best of times.

"GOTCHA!" the eleven year-old shouted with glee, triumphant as she shot her opponent Victoria in the shoulder with a steady stream of water from the barrel of her squirt gun.

Angry and embarrassed, Victoria denied it adamantly, declaring, "You missed!"

Erika exploded with laughter. "Did not! Look at your shirt, you Drip!"

The other girls looked and laughed.

Victoria looked, too. It was soaking wet. She snorted and then swerved away, banking her bicycle in the opposite direction, preparing for another pass at Erika.

Erika banked and maneuvered into another approach position as well. The girls were like two fighter jet pilots as they maneuvered their pedal-driven, two-wheelers in sharp and elongated circles in the middle of the tree-lined, summer street with their friends following close behind, each preparing for another pass. Neighborhood adversaries since they were young enough to remember each other, Victoria was always jealous of the quiet and reserved Erika, and was always trying to outdo her. Victoria she was; victorious she wasn't. Erika's school grades were always higher than hers. Erika was liked by nearly everyone; even Victoria's friends. Even after Erika's long, several months stay in the hospital late last year, Victoria was no less jealous than before. It had been as if Erika had simply just gone away on a long trip to somewhere and then returned one day - with no hair on her head. The reality that Erika was dealing with a life-threatening disease had never found its way into Victoria's world.

Behind them several of their friends were also playing squirt gun tag on wheels. They were loosely assembled on opposing sides: Melanie, Josephine, and Anna were with Erika; Kasey and Toni were with Victoria. For each of them, this was a fun way to pass a few minutes of the hot, summer day. For Victoria, it was a major matter of pride.

Erika and Victoria were now rolling towards each other. They pumped their pedals hard and their bicycles gained speed. The wind blew through Erika's white baseball cap as her bicycle moved faster. Like modern-day medieval knights jousting in the street, squirt guns instead of lances in hand, Erika and Victoria proceeded toward each other, faster and faster. Everyone, except grim-faced Victoria, was enjoying the hot summer day, the cool of the water, and the thrill of the game. Victoria was upset; her eleven year-old pride dented. Her long, curly hair that she had tied back with a scünci whipped back and forth as she pedaled harder. She thought the whole world was laughing at her, because she hadn't gotten Erika Reisling wet. Not even once.

The girls were not the only ones watching the activity in the street. From beneath the cool shade of an oak tree in the Reisling's front yard, Erika's Old English sheepdog, Mooflee, watched with interest as the group of children glided across the pavement toward each other on their bicycles. It was a clear, blue sky summer day on the suburban, tree-lined, Canandaigua street. Summer vacation was in full swing. Mooflee liked summer vacation because the children were all home then and they spent more time playing with her. Her wet, happy tongue dangling from her mouth and her big, brown cow eyes, hidden by tufts of overgrown white hair, followed the pedal-powered, jousting knights as they zoomed passed each other. Her cow eyes then caught sight of the streams of water shooting through the air from the squirt guns.

"Gotcha again!" Erika cheered.

"No, you didn't!" Victoria cried in disbelief.

The other girls laughed again.

Mooflee had seen this show dozens of times before in summers past and was now beginning to tire of it. Bikes zipping around, doing circles, kids cackling, joyful winners and one sour loser. The burly sheepdog now had something else on her mind. With the children occupied, this would be a good time to sneak away. She yawned, innocently stretched out her big, fuzzy legs in front of her, and then, with her large furry paws, she pushed her bulky white and gray body off the ground. Rising from her grassy spot under the old oak, she quietly walked away, heading for the backyard, unnoticed by anyone.

The sheepdog wandered along the side of the Reisling house and into their small backyard. She then strolled toward the thick, tall hedgerow that separated the Reisling's property from their neighbors, the McGillacuddy's. She stopped by a small, thin opening in the hedge. She looked right. She looked left. She then looked behind her and glanced at the Reisling house. Twisting her head further around and shaking the hair momentarily out of her field of view, she looked up at the Reisling tree house. The tree house was perched on a couple of giant limbs, half way up the trunk of the old maple that resided in the middle of the backyard. People were nowhere to be found. Mooflee then eyed the hedgerow through her white tufts of hair which covered those big, brown eyes. The hedgerow was tall, nearly seven feet high, and formed a thick, nearly impenetrable barrier between the properties. Not quite airtight, the hedge did contain many small openings. Mooflee knew of these secret weaknesses in the hedge and stuck her nose in through one such opening.

The sheepdog surveyed the huge, expansive grounds on the other side. The McGillacuddy's estate was incredibly huge and beautiful. It was the finest estate in the county. The grounds behind the mansion were entirely covered with a vast variety of manicured gardens and a network of narrow stone walkways connecting them. Flowers of every conceivable color, shape, and size flourished in the spacious gardens. Statues of Roman figures and elegant water fountains were meticulously placed throughout the gardens. Above the gardens sat the enormous, old Victorian mansion where the McGillacuddys resided. The first floor of the ominous, three-story structure was surrounded on two sides by a large, covered terrace which overlooked the magnificent grounds. The terrace was the prime place to view the colors of the gardens that lay before it. The property's origins dated back over one hundred years and was the finest home old money could buy. It seemed completely out of place, surrounded as it was by the countless - tiny by comparison - middle-class houses, like the Reislings, that made up the neighborhood; all crowded and squeezed in beside it. The neighborhood had simply grown up all around it over the decades. One by one the old mansions of a bygone era had disappeared from the town and only the McGillacuddy's remained.

Every day the estate's owners, Mr. and Mrs. McGillacuddy, could be found lounging there on the terrace, enjoying the beauty of their well-tended backyard.

But they weren't there now.

Mooflee peered up through her shaggy hair at the old Victorian house's terrace and saw no one. The backyard was completely deserted of humans. There wasn't even a single gardener to be seen. With the coast clear, the venturous sheepdog pushed her big, furry body through the opening in the thick hedgerow and crossed into dangerously forbidden territory. She very well knew that dogs were forbidden on the McGillacuddy's property. Despite the danger that lurked, Mooflee pressed on. She knew it was worth the risk.

Back in the street there was a break in the squirt gun action. Erika noticed her dog was no longer there.

"Where'd Mooflee go?" she asked Melanie.

"I saw her walk away just a minute ago," Melanie answered.

"Oh-oh," Erika said.

Erika rode her bicycle into her driveway, stopped, and climbed off.

With a spiteful tone, Victoria called after her. "Where ya goin', Reisling? You're not quittin', are ya?"

"I've got to find my dog."

"Right! Quitter!" Victoria yelled.

"Wet-head!" Erika chided as she left them behind for the backyard.

Victoria could only grumble, but she knew she'd get even with Erika some other time.

Erika walked briskly and took a shortcut to the backyard through the Reisling's garage. She had nothing but Mooflee on her mind. For the last few weeks the loveable dog had been occasionally wandering over to the McGillacuddy's for some unknown reason. She knew how mean and awful Mrs. McGillacuddy could be to her parents about it and she wanted to avoid a scene.

3

Erika suddenly felt lightheaded. Dizziness was followed by a feeling of nausea and she felt sick to her stomach. She stumbled, but quickly regained her balance. She sat down on the garage doorstep and paused to catch her breath. She closed her blue eyes and waited for the world to stop turning, thinking all the while that maybe she had played a little too hard; exerted herself a little too much.

She remembered her doctor's words during her last weekly visit. "Don't over do it, Erika," he had cautioned.

"Hmm," she grunted, sitting on the garage doorstep.

It was during moments like these that Erika was rudely reminded of the disease inside her. The pain it caused; the change in her life; the change in her appearance. She was still pretty; her face soft; her features light. She would lament about the pretty, long, light-brown hair she once had, and wish for its return.

Oh, well. The dizziness would pass. It had before, she reasoned. A few moments later it did pass. The world stopped turning and she felt normal again. Erika stood up and continued toward the backyard.

Beneath an old pine tree on the other side of the hedgerow, Mooflee was eagerly digging a hole with her front paws. A few moments later she had found her treasure: a one-inch thick tenderloin steak! Mooflee drooled as she removed the last few paw-fulls of dirt and then pushed her fuzzy snout into the hole to latch onto the prime cut of beef with her teeth.

When she didn't see her dog, Erika headed for the hole in the hedgerow. This was not the first time Mooflee had crossed the property line and Erika had a good idea where to look. As she approached the opening in the hedge, she could barely make out Mooflee's furry shape on the other side. It looked like she was digging, but Erika couldn't be sure.

"Mooflee, you shouldn't be there," she said to herself. She called out, "Mooflee!"

Just then Erika's eyes caught the movement of something else on the other side of the hedge.

Mooflee heard Erika's voice but ignored it as she closed her jaws on the juicy steak. Erika could wait. The mouth-watering piece of beef could not. Mooflee had barely pulled the steak out of its hole with her teeth when...

WHOOOSH-THUD!!

A garden rake slammed onto the ground right in front of her nose!! Startled, Mooflee dropped the steak. The dog yelped and jumped back. The steak fell back into the shallow hole. She then looked up. There stood an old woman dressed in red. It was the old woman who owned the property. She was motionless as she leered angrily at Mooflee. Her head was large; her intense eyes were wide set and faded blue. Her hair was shoulder-length and grizzled brown.

The old woman hissed and raised the garden rake to strike again.

Frightened, Mooflee whined and ran away, leaping through the hole in the hedgerow. Leaves from the hedge flew everywhere.

Mrs. McGillacuddy's loud, raspy voice yelled, "And don't you come back, you mangy, low-life mutt!" The weathered wrinkles on her face, a result of too many years of cigarette smoking and from the stress associated with being a nasty human being, fluttered with vengeance. Her longish hair, an attempt to make her look younger than her sixty years would allow, whipped uncontrollably through the air as she shouted.

Erika was running to the hedgerow by this time. She could just make out Mrs. M standing there in her red dress.

"Hey, don't you hurt my dog, Mrs. McGillacuddy!" she yelled.

Mooflee ran to Erika. The girl kneeled and took the dog in her arms. Mooflee was glad to see her Erika and licked her face.

Mrs. McGillacuddy shook her rake at both of them. "I'm warning you, you little brat! I don't like your dog coming over here and burying his food. You keep that animal off my property or else I'll have it taken away!" She then called out to her gardener to come and clean up the mess beside the hedgerow.

Erika hugged her dog and noticed how scared she was. "Mooflee, you're shivering." To Mrs. McGillacuddy, she shouted, "How could you be so mean?"

Mrs. McGillacuddy was appalled by what she perceived as a cavalier remark from an impudent little child. Angry red veins popped out on her forehead and her face looked like it was going to explode. She snapped, "And if you ever talk back to me again, I'll have *you* taken away, too, little girl."

She then abruptly turned, held her head high, and strutted away with rake in hand. She reminded Erika of some picture she had seen of a red devil carrying a pitchfork.

"She's a meany, isn't she, Mooflee? Are you all right?" Erika asked as she petted the dog. "What a witch she is. Did the witchy-poo scare you? Someday she'll get hers, won't she?"

Mooflee stopped shivering and licked Erika's face again with approval.

Melanie, Josephine, and Anna arrived just then. "What happened?" they asked.

Nodding toward her next-door neighbor, Erika said, "McGilla Gorilla tried to hit Mooflee with a rake."

"She what?!" Jo asked, surprised.

A voice from above and behind shouted, "She did! I saw it. She tried to hit Mooflee with a rake!"

All four girls turned around to look. Up in the Reisling tree house, a little boy was emerging and climbing down the makeshift wooden ladder.

"Johnny Ingle, what are you doing up there in our tree house?" Erika called to him.

"I was waiting for Michele to come up and play," the boy replied. He skipped the last two steps on the wooden ladder and jumped to the ground.

"You know you're not supposed to play up there by yourself," Erika scolded him.

"Oh, okay," the five year old said with disappointment, as he approached the girls.

"Yeah," Jo added, "were you invited?"

"Well, no; but it's a cool tree house!" little Johnny said with enthusiasm.

Erika said, "Go find Michele and *then* you can play up there."

"Okay!" the little boy said, and he zoomed off.

Looking at the McGillacuddy's, Anna shook her head and said, "That rotten woman. She's despicable."

"You should tell your parents what 'Mil-Dread' did," Melanie asserted.

Erika looked at her happy, cow-eyed sheepdog and said, "I'm going to."

Mooflee barked. She wholeheartedly agreed.

DINNER

Mooflee lay on the floor beside the dinner table as the Reislings ate. Her eyes were closed, but her ears were as alert as sonar, listening for the most miniscule morsel of food that might drop to the wooden floor. She was standing by for clean up.

"Dad, can't we call the sheriff?" Erika asked.

"No, honey. It wouldn't do any good. She's just a grumpy old woman."

Mrs. Reisling looked at her husband and added, "She's a spoiled and arrogant woman. That's what she is, Rick."

Mr. Reisling nodded in agreement.

"Besides, Mooflee wasn't hurt," he said to his daughter. "She's all right."

Mr. Reisling glanced at the sheepdog who, upon hearing her name, raised her head as though she had been called. Her tongue was happily hanging out of her mouth and she was panting. The thought of an impending juicy handout was crossing her mind and making her drool.

"Does she have to get hurt first before we can call the sheriff?" Erika asked.

"No, of course not, Erika. Mrs. McGillacuddy was probably just trying to scare Mooflee, that's all."

"No, Dad, she wasn't. She was definitely trying to *hit* Mooflee. If Mooflee hadn't jumped out of the way, she would have been hurt. She also called me a brat and said she'd have *me* taken away the next time I spoke to her."

"She did?" Mrs. Reisling asked, surprised.

"Yes."

Mr. Reisling asked, "What did you say to her, Sweetheart?"

"I told her it was a mean thing she did to my dog."

Mrs. Reisling looked at Mr. Reisling with anger. "Rick, that woman is really becoming obnoxious. How dare she say something like that to Erika. Just because she's wealthy doesn't give her the right to talk to our child that way."

"She's got some nerve," Mr. Reisling said. "I'll call her after dinner and have a few words with her." Erika could see her dad was suddenly upset.

"After you talk to her, can you then call the sheriff?" Erika persisted.

Mrs. Reisling said to her daughter, "Honey, I know how you feel. I don't like the McGillacuddy's either."

Erika couldn't hold it in any more and she raised her voice. "They're snobs! Arrogant, uncaring, selfish snobs!"

"Yeah! Snobs!" Michele chimed in, providing additional support to her big sister's cause. She then looked at her sister and said, "Erika? Who are you talking about?"

"Erika, that's not nice," Mr. Reisling said.

"Sorry."

"No, it isn't nice..." Mrs. Reisling added, "...but it's true. Those people are the most un-neighborly people I've ever lived next to in my whole life. She thinks her neighbors are too blue collar for her blue blood."

"Does she really have blue blood, Mom?" Michele asked.

"No, Michele. It's just an expression," Mrs. Reisling assured her. To her husband, she said, "I've tried to be pleasant with them. Remember the first day we moved in?"

Mr. Reisling nodded. "Yes, I remember."

"I went over to introduce myself and I had a tray of home-baked, chocolate-chip cookies to give her."

"She slammed the door in her face," Mr. Reisling said to his daughters, finishing the story.

Mrs. Reisling said, "Erika, they've never gotten along with anyone in the neighborhood, and they probably never will. We just have to make sure Mooflee stays off their property."

"I wonder why she goes over there?" Mr. Reisling asked.

Erika answered, "She was digging for something when I found her."

"Digging for what?"

"I don't know, Dad," was all Erika could say.

Only Mooflee, lying there on the floor waiting for morsels of food to drop off the dinner table, knew the answer. And she wasn't telling.

THE TELEPHONE CALL

Mrs. Reisling washed the dinner dishes as she watched her husband pace back and forth on the kitchen floor with the telephone in his hand. He was upset - an unusual characteristic for him - as he spoke with Mrs. McGillacuddy. Mr. Reisling was a diplomatic individual who tried to be fair with everyone. Obviously, the conversation was not going as hoped.

"I'm sorry she wandered over there, Mrs. McGillacuddy," Mr. Reisling was saying. "All I'm asking is that in the future you simply call us if you should see her over there again. That's all. She's not a vicious dog. She's not going to hurt anybody. There's no need to swing rakes and possibly injure the dog, and perhaps yourself. (pause) I understand that, Mrs. McGillacuddy. I *know* it's your property... (pause) Yes...I understand..."

Suddenly diplomatic patience went out the window.

"Listen, Mrs. McGillacuddy. My daughter is no brat. She's a sweet little girl and if you had ever taken the time to talk to her nicely, you'd know that. She also happens to be a sick little girl." There was a pause. "I know she doesn't look sick, but she is. She was getting chemotherapy throughout the entire winter. Now, the next time you threaten her - are you listening? - the next time you threaten her, *I'll* call the sheriff on *you.* Do *you* understand *that?* Hello?"

She had hung up.

He stood there for an empty moment and then looked at his wife.

"That went...well," Mrs. Reisling said.

Mr. Reisling sighed with frustration as he set the telephone down on the table. He said, "I can't believe it. I got angry. I actually let myself get angry."

Mrs. Reisling shook her head as she washed dishes and said, "She's an impossible person. I'd say that was a normal reaction."

Erika lay on Michele's bed reading her five-year-old sister a bedtime story. The story was Michele's favorite, *Hillary's Wish*, and she was totally absorbed in her big sister's reading of it. Mooflee lay beside Michele's bed on the floor listening, too, while Erika read.

"'Who-who's Heno?,' Hillary asked," Erika read, changing the tone of her voice with each character. "'The librarian answered, 'Heno. He is the Seneca Spirit of Thunder. They say he rides the angry skies, throwing his fiery bolts. He purifies the water and chases away trespassers from sacred grounds.' 'What's he look like?' Amy asked. The librarian laughed. 'Ha! What's he look like? Oh, don't worry about that. You'll know him when you see him.'"

Just then their dad stepped into the room. "Hi, girls."

Both girls responded, "Hi, Dad."

"Watcha reading?"

"*Hillary's Wish*," Erika answered.

"That's a good story. My mom used to read it to me."

"Your mom read you bedtime stories, Daddy?" Michele asked.

"Every night." He looked at Erika and said, "Listen, Sweetheart, the next time Mrs. McGillacuddy says anything to you, just ignore her and don't say anything back to her. And then come and tell us. Okay?"

"Okay, Dad. She wasn't very friendly to you on the phone, was she?"

"No. She wasn't."

"What's wrong with her?" Erika asked. "Does she have a brain disease?"

"I don't know. She's just one very unhappy person."

"Maybe she should watch Nickelodeon, even though it's just for kids," Michele suggested. "That'll make her happy."

Mr. Reisling smiled. "Maybe it would, Michele. I'll tell her you said so the next time I speak to her."

Erika took the thought a step further. "Maybe she should watch *The Wizard of Oz* and see what happens to the Wicked Witch of the West."

"Erika..." Mr. Reisling cautioned.

"Sorry, Dad. I guess 'one should not fault a blind man for being unable to see.'"

"Hmm. That's one way of putting it," her dad said. "Well, good-night, girls." Mr. Reisling leaned over both his daughters and gave them each a kiss. "I love you both."

"Good night, Dad," the two sisters said.

Mr. Reisling rose from the bed and then reached down and petted Mooflee. "Good night, you trouble maker." As he headed for the door he stopped and said, "Oh, Erika, don't forget, you have your appointment with Doctor Mervis tomorrow."

"That's great!" Michele said. "I like his playroom."

"I'm glad, 'Chele," Erika said blandly. "Okay, Dad."

Her father smiled and then quietly left the room, leaving the door slightly ajar.

There was a part of Erika that didn't really want to go to see Doctor Mervis. After all, she was fine now. She was playing just like any of the other kids in the neighborhood. She wasn't sick. But another part of her knew she *had* to go. Just to make sure the bad blood cells weren't coming back.

"Erika, where do you learn all those sayings?" Michele asked.

"What sayings?"

"You know, like the thing you just said to dad about the 'blind man'?"

"Oh. From books. From lots and lots of reading. Well, it's time for me to go to bed, Sis."

Erika leapt from the bed and then sat down on the floor for a moment beside Mooflee. Michele leaned her head over the side of the bed and peered down at them. Erika hugged her dog and pulled the hair back from over Mooflee's big eyes.

"What big eyes you have, Grandma," Michele giggled.

"Don't worry, Mooflee. I'll never let anything happen to you. Just don't go over to McGilla Gorilla's house anymore, you big moose," Erika said, giving the dog a noogee with her knuckle. "Okay?"

Michele giggled and said to the dog, "Good-night, Moosey."

The big sheepdog held her head high, her tongue hanging out, and smiled at all of the attention she was receiving from her two best friends. Michele looked at her sister and they both giggled.

THE WEEKLY DOCTOR'S VISIT

The next day Mrs. Reisling and Michele drove Erika to her weekly doctor's appointment at the Strong Memorial Hospital. Ever since her leukemia had slipped into remission last winter, she had been placed on the weekly maintenance program. Besides the usual physical exam given by the doctor, the program included the drawing of her blood for testing to see if any bad cells had returned. Once that was completed, she was given chemotherapy through the catheter that had been implanted in the upper right side of her chest. The indwelling catheter, as it was called, had a short, eight-inch plastic tube attached to it and when not in use was cleaned and coiled and taped to her skin. The coiled tubing against her chest caused a slight bulge when she wore a T-shirt or swimsuit, but it did not cause her any pain or discomfort. To Erika, who had long since become accustomed to it, it was just a little tube that came out of her body. The catheter and tubing provided a permanent way for the nurses to administer Erika's weekly treatments so she wouldn't have to endure the pain of being poked in the arm with a sharp needle every week or the risk of infection. On the inside of her body the catheter was connected to another small tube which led directly to her vein. So far the program was working, her platelet count had been good, and her leukemia stayed in remission. Erika liked to think her disease was sleeping and this allowed her to be healthy.

Michele was left in the hospital's playroom. She happily played with the toys and the other children who were waiting for family members while Erika and her mom went in to see Doctor Mervis.

Erika liked Doctor Mervis. He was a small, soft-spoken man with thick, black hair and brown eyes. He was kind and overflowing with patience. He always seemed to have all of the time in the world for her, unlike other doctors she had met in the past who merely flew in through the door to the examining room, glanced at a clipboard to remember her name, performed a quick exam, and then flew out the door again without so much as saying a word. Even though she didn't like or want to go to the hospital every week at first, Erika slowly changed her mind and began to look forward to it. Going to Doctor Mervis's was always a pleasant, relaxing time for her; but, much more than that, she trusted him. Doctor Mervis had successfully treated her throughout the fall and winter and, as a result, had saved her life.

The examination went well. Doctor Mervis talked to Erika while Mrs. Reisling looked on. Mrs. Reisling greatly appreciated Doctor Mervis's light, upbeat way with children.

"So...how do you feel?" he asked.

"Good," Erika responded.

"Are you having a fun summer?"

"Yes. So far, so good."

"I'm glad. What are you doing with yourself?"

"I'm playing with Mooflee, my dog."

"What type of dog is he? Or is it a she?" Doctor Mervis asked.

"She's an Old English sheepdog," Erika answered.

"Oh, they're lots of fun. What else have you been doing?"

"I ride my bicycle and swim in the lake with my friends. The stuff I always do," Erika said proudly. "I don't feel ill at all."

Doctor Mervis nodded. He noticed the independence in her voice.

Erika added with some bravado, "No disease is going to stop me."

"Do you feel tired?" he asked.

"Sometimes. A little," she admitted.

"Uh-huh."

Just then Nurse Bright appeared and prepared to extract a blood sample from the catheter implanted in Erika's chest.

"Okay, relax now, Erika, while Nurse Bright takes your blood. This will only take a minute."

"I'm not scared, Doctor Mervis. I know you want to check my blood to see how my white count is doing. This isn't my first time, you know," she reminded him.

"I know, Erika. I'm sorry. I know you're not scared. You've never been scared. You're my bravest patient. Not all of my patients are as brave as you," Doctor Mervis said as the nurse inserted the needle into the catheter. Erika didn't even flinch.

Erika continued. "We want to make sure those nasty bad cells aren't coming back."

"That's right," Doctor Mervis said as Nurse Bright withdrew the sample of blood into the small collection vial. He smiled and looked at Erika's mom. "Well, Mrs. Reisling, I should be careful about telling Erika too much. Next thing you know she'll be wanting my job."

"I'd like that job. I'd get to help kids," Erika said with a sense of purpose.

After they had finished the exam, Doctor Mervis said, "Nurse Bright explained to me that you won't be waiting for the results today. Is that right?"

"Yes," Mrs. Reisling said. "Erika doesn't want to be late for her friend's birthday party on the lake."

He nodded, and then handed Erika a small red rose. "For my bravest patient. This is for you," he said.

"Oh, thank you, Doctor Mervis," Erika said with joy. "It's beautiful."

"You're welcome, Erika. I want you to have a very nice week. Okay?"

"I will. Bye, Doctor Mervis. See you next time," Erika said. "I'll be in the playroom with Michele."

"Bye-bye, Erika."

Erika dashed out of the examination room, her sneakers pounding the floor as though she were in an elementary school gymnasium and not a doctor's office. Mrs. Reisling and Doctor Mervis watched her leave. Nurse Bright followed with an I.V. stand.

"She seems different, doesn't she?" Mrs. Reisling asked as she watched her daughter run to play.

Doctor Mervis nodded. "I noticed the change. I think she's having trouble adjusting to the fact that it's not over, even though it seems like it is, and that she may be sick again."

Mrs. Reisling nodded. "She plays very hard. She plays so hard it's almost like, like...an act of denial. Yet, I don't wish to restrain her."

"It's good that she's active while she's adjusting. I'd trust her to know when too much is enough. I wouldn't worry about it; but I would like to make a suggestion, if I may."

"No, not at all. What is it?"

"Have you or your husband talked about taking her to the camp I mentioned?"

"Not recently. Why? Do you think it still would be a good idea?"

Doctor Mervis said, "She'd meet other kids who have gone through what she has. It could help."

Mrs. Reisling nodded. "We'll give it some thought. Thanks, Doctor Mervis."

"You're welcome," he said as he turned to leave. "I'll give you a call when the test results come back."

"Okay," Mrs. Reisling said appreciatively. "Thank you."

In the playroom, Erika and Michele were sitting at a table playing the card game *Uno*.

"Mooflee would have fun in this place," Michele noted. "Can we bring her next time?"

"I don't think so, 'Chele," Erika said as she studied her cards. "Dogs aren't allowed in hospitals."

Nurse Bright entered and positioned the I.V. stand next to Erika. Attached to the top of the I.V. stand, a clear plastic bag was hanging from it. The bag contained the necessary drug for killing the bad cells in her blood. Dangling from the bag was a long, narrow plastic tube. Michele watched as her sister unbuttoned her shirt and Nurse Bright connected the end of the narrow tube to the catheter in her chest. A moment later Nurse Bright opened a little wheeled valve beneath the bag and the drug began flowing slowly into Erika's veins.

"Erika, does that hurt?" Michele asked.

"No, not at all," her sister answered as she looked over her hand of *Uno* cards.

"Can you *taste* it?"

"No, of course not. Come on. Quit asking silly questions and let's play."

PEGGY'S BIRTHDAY PARTY

Once home from the hospital, Erika dashed to her bedroom and put on her swimsuit. The swimsuit was a one-piece and provided a means for her to hide and protect her catheter and tubing. Even though the hospital strongly recommended against kids with catheters going swimming due to the risk of bacteria in pools and lakes, many did, anyway, and Erika was no exception. As long as she washed and cleaned it when she returned from the beach, her parents allowed her to swim.

She then threw on some tan shorts and a peach-colored T-shirt. She stood in front of the vanity mirror in her bedroom as she dressed. She then took a moment to look at her hairless head. She leaned toward the mirror and studied her head for any signs of new hair growth. Doctor Mervis had told her not to expect it to return for as long as a year and, of course, he was right. There wasn't a single hair to be found. It had been that way ever since she had begun chemotherapy in the fall. Her purple hairbrush still sat on the vanity, patiently waiting to be used again. She then walked over to her hat rack in the corner and picked out one of her cutesy hats. A red, floppy one with a magenta brim.

Modeling it for herself in front of the vanity mirror, she decided she wasn't entirely happy with the way it looked because it didn't quite work with the light summer attire of tan shorts and the peach-colored T-shirt she was wearing. She took the hat off and tossed it onto the hat rack. It snagged one of the rack's pegs and stayed. The only hat she owned that would fashionably work was her white baseball cap. She walked over to the hat rack again and fetched the white cap.

Just then she heard a knock downstairs at the kitchen door and she knew it was Mel and Jo. She placed the hat on her head, dashed out of her room, and ran down the stairs.

Racing through the kitchen, her mom asked, "Do you have Peggy's present?"

"Yes, Mom. Right here," she answered, grabbing her backpack off the counter and heading for the door. "See you later."

"Bye, Sweetie," Mrs. Reisling said. She followed her daughter outside. "Be careful riding to the beach."

"I will."

Erika and her friends climbed onto their bicycles and rode down the driveway.

"You girls have fun," Mrs. Reisling called out.

"We will, Mrs. Reisling," Jo called back.

"Thanks, Mrs. Reisling," Melanie added.

"Be sure to help Mrs. Winkleman clean up after the party."

"We will. Bye, Mom," Erika said.

"Bye," Mrs. Reisling said and waved.

16

Mooflee was laying on the front yard. Erika stopped her bike beside her. "You be a good girl. All right?"
The fuzzy sheepdog just smiled and raised her head as if she could see.

Riding out into the street, the three girls noticed a lot of activity going on next door at the McGillacuddy's. Preparations for a big function were well underway. There were a dozen cars parked in front of the big house. A large, white tent with three poles had been erected. Dozens of tables and hundreds of chairs had been set up around the covered terrace that overlooked the gardens. Two large trucks rumbled in haste passed the girls. On the side of both trucks, in strikingly flamboyant calligraphy, were the words, "Fritz's Catering." Beneath it were smaller words that said, "More Glitz with Fritz!" The trucks turned into the McGillacuddy's driveway and drove up to the house.
Melanie asked, "What's going on over there?"
"Just another one of Mrs. McGillacuddy's big deal garden parties for somebody important or something," Erika answered. "She has them all the time."
Jo said, "Look over there."
The girls turned and saw an old man running between the tall, thick oaks which were generously spaced in the McGillacuddy's enormous front grounds. He darted from tree to tree as though he were sneaking up on something. At the same time he was looking around, his head turning and twisting and bobbing up and down in the air like a chicken in tall grass. He was swinging something through the air that went "Whoosh."
"Isn't that Mr. McGillacuddy?" Jo asked.
"Yes, that's him," Erika said.
"What's he doing?" Melanie asked.
Jo added, "He's swatting something."
Erika said, "He's not swatting anything. He's chasing butterflies. That's a butterfly net in his hand."
"Chasing butterflies?" Melanie realized. "Why would anyone want to chase butterflies?"
"I heard he collects them," Erika added. "Let's go."
After the girls had gone, Cecil McGillacuddy's pursuit of a butterfly led him near the hedgerow that separated the Reisling's from the McGillacuddy's. He stopped and peered through an opening in the hedge and saw Mooflee relaxing in the shade of the Reisling's front yard. Cecil took a good long look at the dog and smiled.

On their way to the beach, Erika and her friends encountered Mrs. McGillacuddy's chauffeur-driven limousine. It was returning from town.
"Hey, here comes Mrs. M now," Melanie said.

"Mil-Dread, Mil-Dread," Jo sneered, mocking Mrs. McGillacuddy's first name.

As the car passed, Erika saw Mrs. McGillacuddy sitting gravely in the back seat. She looked at Erika and gave her a searing scowl. Erika couldn't understand how this woman could be so mean all of the time. Erika couldn't restrain herself. She immediately responded to Mrs. McGillacuddy's grim scowl by sticking her tongue out at her. Mrs. McGillacuddy saw it and was instantly outraged. She seethed the rest of the way home.

Erika giggled to herself. "I bet the telephone at my house will be ringing any minute now."

It was a searing, hot afternoon and Kershaw Park was a hub of summer activity when they arrived for Peggy Winkleman's birthday party. The lakefront park was crowded with hundreds of people in search of a place to cool off and the sandy beach was covered with a wide assortment of large, colorful towels and umbrellas. People were in the lake splashing and swimming. Others were playing volleyball while some even had paddleboats on the water. The lifeguards were having a busy day of it. They blew their whistles and scolded young boys who were roughhousing too much.

Erika & Co. found Peggy and her mom, Anna and her mom, and some of their other friends, along with Peggy's little brother, gathered in the picnic area. Peggy's table was covered with a brightly colored tablecloth and party supplies. Bottles of soda, assorted bags of munchies, and two boxes of fresh sheet pizza. Balloons and ribbons were strung between the trees. Peggy's little seven year-old brother Todd was sitting at the food table already and eating. Peggy's mom had wanted to do something different for her daughter's birthday besides the usual party at the house and had decided on having a beach party.

They all greeted each other. Peggy asked, "Did you bring your swimsuits?"

"I'm wearing mine," Erika said.

"Me, too," Melanie and Jo chimed in.

"Good," Peggy said. "Let's go swimming!" To her little brother, she said, "Hey, Todd, leave some pizza for the rest of us."

"I will. There's plenty," the boy said as he continued to stuff his mouth.

Erika, Melanie, and Jo placed their backpacks on one of the picnic tables. They removed their clothes down to their swimsuits and dashed into the lake with the other partygoers. After they had cooled off, they came out of the water and played catch with a Frisbee.

Peggy's mother, Mrs. Winkleman, began to wonder if she had made a mistake having a birthday party on such a scorching day as this, but was soon relieved to see that Peggy and her friends were having a good time. She also noticed the hot day had taken a toll on the ice supply and there wasn't much left to cool the soda.

"Peggy," she said to her daughter, "Anna's mom and I are going to the store across the street to get some more ice. We'll be right back."

"Okay, Mom," Peggy said as she tossed the Frisbee.

The two mothers then left.

Anna looked at Erika and asked, "Did you tell your parents about Mrs. McGillacuddy?"

"What happened?" Peggy asked, puzzled.

Melanie said, "The 'Dread tried to hit Erika's dog with a rake."

"She did? Really?" Peggy was astounded.

Erika said, "Yes. I told my parents and my dad called her."

"What'd she say?" Anna asked.

"She hung up on him," Erika said.

Anna was surprised. "She hung up on your dad? What a witch!"

Erika said, "She threatened to have Mooflee taken away."

"You should tell Doc all about it," Peggy suggested. "He'd have an idea about what to do."

"Is he coming to the party?" Erika asked.

Peggy suddenly moved closer to them and whispered, as though she were sharing a great secret. "He was taken away yesterday."

"What?" Melanie asked.

Anna asked, "Taken away?"

Erika said, "What do you mean? Taken away by who?"

Peggy's eyes darted around the crowded park as she answered in her secretive voice. "By the *government.*"

"The government?" Erika asked out loud. "*Our* country's government?"

"Shhh!" Peggy said. "They drove right to his house and five minutes later he was gone! I saw the whole thing from my driveway."

"What did he do?" Erika asked.

"His mom told my mom that Doc had computer-hacked his way into some top secret government files and got caught. So they took him away. His mom's really upset."

Jo asked, "I wonder what's so 'top secret'? What would *our* government have to hide?"

Erika asked, "Where'd they take him?"

"I think to jail," Peggy said. "Or some unpleasant place where they take people who computer-hack their way into government files. I don't know."

Melanie said, "He probably has to sit in a dungeon and write five-hundred times, 'I shall not hack again.'"

"When's he coming back?" Erika asked.

Peggy said, "Who knows?"

Just then Peggy spotted Victoria and her friends coming towards them.

"Oh-oh," she said. "They weren't invited to my party."

19

Erika and the other girls turned around to look. Victoria was with Kasey and Toni.

"They weren't invited to my party," Peggy repeated.

Tossing the Frisbee to Melanie, Erika said, "Just ignore them. They'll go away."

The girls continued to throw the Frisbee in a circle.

"Hi wimps," Victoria said with arrogance. "Hey, Peggy, why wasn't I was invited to your party, too?"

Defiantly, Peggy said, "Because you weren't, Victoria, so why don't you just buzz off."

Victoria stepped into the middle of circle and snatched the Frisbee out of the air. Being the tallest girl in the circle, she held it high and waved it defiantly above them all. No one bothered attempting to snatch it back from her.

Victoria turned to Erika. "Where'd you losers run off to yesterday?"

"I had to find my dog, Vick-ster," Erika said with sarcasm. "Now, throw the Frisbee here, like a good little girl."

"Yeah, I'll bet you went to find your dog. I bet you just couldn't take getting squirted in the face."

Victoria didn't scare Erika one bit, even if she was two inches taller. She knew Victoria was just a bully with a big mouth. She acted tough, but that was about all.

Erika calmly said, "I didn't get squirted in the face. You did. I guess your empty head doesn't remember that far back in time. Now give me the Frisbee, Victoria, and quit trying to be a bully. You look pretty silly."

"I look silly? Ha! Looks who's talking!" Victoria said as she looked at Erika's hairless, baseball-capped head and then shot a glance down at the small bulge in her bathing suit caused by the catheter and tube.

"That's enough, Victoria!" Melanie said with anger, defending her friend.

"Mind your own business 'Chinny, chin, Chen,'" Victoria blurted out, making fun of Melanie's Asian last name.

"Leave them alone!" Jo chimed in.

"You're a real dummy, Victoria," Anna added with disdain.

"Why don't you get out of here," Peggy demanded.

Erika was unfazed. "It's okay. Don't worry about it. Victoria doesn't have a clue what it means. She's too ignorant to learn why I have no hair."

"I don't care about your weird looks, Riesling. You want your stupid Frisbee? Go get it!" Victoria grunted as she flung the Frisbee into the air.

The Frisbee flew high over their heads, just out of reach. It came down fast and hard, hitting Peggy's brother Todd who was still sitting beside the food at the picnic table. He was drinking grape Kool-Aid when the Frisbee slammed into his cup and splashed the liquid all over his face and his bright, white T-shirt. Victoria laughed out loud and uttered an impish "Ooops."

"Hey! Look what you did!" the seven year-old yelled in protest.

As Victoria continued to laugh, Todd gave her a look that would have singed the bark off a tree. He instantly looked for something to throw at her. Spying the sheet of pizza before him, he grabbed a slice and hurled it through the air. Caught completely by surprise, it hit Victoria square on the side of the face. This put a sudden end to her annoying cackling.

What happened next was a chain-reaction.

Victoria picked the remains of the pizza off her face and threw it back at Todd. Unfortunately, she missed and hit Anna instead. Anna shrieked and whipped her paper cup of Coke-Cola at Victoria. She missed and the soda splattered all over Melanie.

"Hey!" Melanie cried out angrily.

Victoria roared with laughter.

Melanie ran to the picnic table, grabbed a slice of pizza, and threw it at Victoria.

"Hey, stop it girls!" Peggy yelled. "Leave the food alone. Cut it out!"

Melanie missed and hit Victoria's friend Kasey instead. Not thinking it one bit funny, Kasey threw it back at Melanie. Melanie leaned to the left and the slice of pizza hit Erika in the face.

"Stop it!" Peggy yelled. "That's enough!"

Angered, Erika ran to the picnic table and grabbed a plastic bottle of ketchup. She aimed it at Victoria and gave it a hefty squeeze, but nothing happened. The top was clogged with a dried-up glob of ketchup. Victoria laughed out loud.

Just then Peggy's and Anna's moms returned from the store with a couple of large bags of ice. They were talking to each other and were unaware of the food fight. Erika continued squeezing the bottle as hard as she could with all of her strength. Suddenly, the dried up glob shot off the top like a bullet and dark, red ketchup exploded from the bottle, sending a long streak of red stuff shooting through the air. Victoria instantly saw it coming and jumped out of the way just in time, but Peggy's mom, who was walking up from behind her and talking with Anna's mom, didn't see it. It splattered her in the face and dripped down the front of her shirt and all over the bag of ice.

"Uh-oh," Erika said.

Victoria snickered and said, "Big 'uh-oh.' Come on, girls. Let's split the scene."

Victoria, Kasey, and Toni then took haste and fled.

REISLING HOME

After the beach party Erika, Melanie, and Josephine rode their bikes home. An afternoon of swimming had cleansed their swimsuits of food stains and the ride home dried them off in the sunshine and the fresh passing air.

"Boy, Erika, you're lucky Mrs. Winkleman is such a nice lady, otherwise you'd be in big trouble," Melanie said.

"I know. But, hey, I didn't start it. Victoria did."

"It's a good thing it was a hot day," Jo added. "Mrs. Winkleman didn't mind jumping in the lake to clean the ketchup off her shirt."

"Did you see the look on her face when the ketchup hit her?" Melanie asked. The girls laughed.

"I didn't know ketchup could fly that far," Jo said.

"Me neither," Erika added, and giggled some more.

"Why do you put up with jerky Victoria, anyway, Erika?" Melanie asked.

"Yeah," Jo said. "Why don't you just smack her?"

"I just don't believe in kicking a stupid person because they're stupid. Besides, she's just all talk."

"Still, somebody ought to straighten her out," Melanie said.

When they turned into Erika's driveway, the girls saw more cars parked in front of the McGillacuddy mansion than when they had left. They could hear the sounds of a large crowd and music going on in the spacious grounds.

"Looks like McGilla Gorilla's garden party is in full swing," Melanie observed.

Erika said, "Let's go see who's at this one."

Mooflee was lying in the garage and jumped up when she heard Erika.

"Hi, Moof," Erika said when the dog ran out to greet her.

They dropped their bikes, petted the dog, and then ran out to the Reisling's backyard. Mooflee followed. The trio dropped to the ground and crawled to the hedgerow where they could peek through the branches to watch. Mooflee wiggled her way in between them.

The garden party was a big event. Nicely dressed men in three-piece suits and elegant women filled the garden and terrace areas. Everyone was either talking, drinking, or eating. Servers were everywhere carrying large trays of hors d'oeuvres to the guests. A buffet table had been set up just below the terrace and a long line of people flowed passed it filling their plates with delicacies. An elegantly dressed young woman seated off by herself on the terrace played a large harp, providing background music.

The girls then saw Mrs. McGillacuddy. Standing near the harpist, she was marshaling her husband to have more hors d'oeuvres brought in. As they watched through the hedgerow, each of the girls had a different image of the notorious woman in their minds.

"There's Mrs. McGillacuddy up there on the porch bullying Cecil," Erika said. To her, Mrs. "McGilla-gorilla" was an angry, blustering primate swatting her husband with a heavy, cosmetics-laden handbag.

"Poor guy. She never leaves him alone," Melanie added. Mel saw Mrs. McGillacuddy as an ugly, long-nosed witch, busy stirring a steaming stew with a paddle in a large, black cauldron with her husband standing helplessly in the middle of it.

Jo saw Mrs. McGillacuddy as a miserable giant towering over her mansion and gardens, like the central character in the film "Attack of the Fifty-foot Woman," bellowing orders down to her dwarfish husband who was cowering beneath the buffet table.

Even Mooflee spotted Mrs. McGillacuddy through the hair over her eyes and growled.

"Shhhh, Moof," Erika said, placing an arm around the dog to comfort her.

Mooflee imagined Mrs. McGillacuddy as an ugly, teeth-baring, flesh-spitting Doberman or schipperke biting at Mr. McGillacuddy's backside, shredding his pants.

The girls then recognized some of the McGillacuddy's important guests.

"There's Helen Hunt! She's a movie star," Melanie whispered excitedly. "I can't believe she's here right next door to your house!"

"There's Roma Downey, the TV star!" Erika pointed out.

Through her hairy, fuzzy face, Mooflee was stunned to see an attractive sheepdog. The girls noticed this, too, and were just as surprised.

"Wow," Jo said. "Someone actually brought a dog to one of Mrs. McGillacuddy's parties.

"Where?" Erika asked.

"Over there. By the harp player."

Melanie said, "It's a sheepdog, just like Mooflee."

"I can't believe it." Erika was astounded when she spotted the dog.

She then watched as Mr. McGillacuddy walked over to the dog, handed it a slice of meat, and then knelt down and gave the dog a big hug.

"Did you see that? Do you believe that? Mrs. McGillacuddy would swing a rake at our sheepdog, but that sheepdog is treated like royalty."

Jo said, "The owners must be *really* special people for the McGillacuddys to tolerate them bringing their dog."

"What phonies they are," Erika said. "If only their friends really knew how they behaved towards animals."

Erika & Co. continued to observe Mr. McGillacuddy. He was having difficulty navigating a straight course in the garden.

"Cecil's drunk," Melanie observed.

He veered to the right and then staggered to the left, and then was pricked on the leg when he walked into a sharp, thorny rose bush. His eyes bugged out for a second and he instantly jumped backwards several feet, barely missing a collision with one of his lady guests. Erika & Co. covered their mouths to contain their laughter.

Mr. McGillacuddy then quickly looked around to see if anyone had noticed his accident. Most everyone had seen it, but politely pretended they hadn't.

The girls then saw Mrs. McGillacuddy stroll close to their hiding spot in the hedge. They could overhear her talking to one of her lady guests.

The guest said, "It's a lovely party, Mildred, and you're home is lovely, too. And your gardens...they're breathtaking."

"Thank you," Mrs. McGillacuddy said, and smiled.

"And you have *so* many neighbors," the woman continued as she surveyed the ground's perimeter. "Who are your neighbors, by the way?" she asked, gesturing toward the Reisling property.

Mrs. McGillacuddy answered with a carefree wave of her hand, "Nobody important. Just some mundane couple with their bratty little child and awful dog."

The girls were appalled. Melanie said, "Did you hear that?"

"What an arrogant witch!" Erika whispered, grinding her teeth, as the witch shared a toast with the woman. "Boy, I'd like to throw a 'mundane' slice of pizza at her."

"I've got something better," Melanie said as she calmly pulled a nerf gun from her pocket and loaded a small piece of chewing gum onto its tip.

"What are you doing?" Erika asked.

Without answering, Melanie drew a deep breath and blew it at the witch. It missed, however, and hit a well-dressed man instead. Thinking he had been rammed by a big, flying bug, the man slapped the back of his head as though he were swatting a mosquito. This drove the piece of gum deep into the man's hair where it became firmly lodged.

The girls giggled as the man tried to dig around and remove the mysterious object that was matting his scalp. Finally locating it, the man pulled at it and unknowingly stretched a foot-long stringy line of the chewy substance from the back of his head which promptly snapped and fell on the shoulder of his dress jacket.

The girls giggled hysterically and bit their lips to keep from being heard.

The man finally noticed something stuck to his hand and tried to shake it off by whipping his wrist back and forth. In the process he accidentally bumped into a waitress, causing her to spill her tray of champagne flutes.

The girls giggled louder, almost uncontrollably. The loud din of breaking glass masked their snickering.

"Shh-shh!" Erika whispered with limited control.

Mrs. McGillacuddy shot a gaze in their direction.

Melanie whispered, "She's looking this way."

"Come on. Let's scram," Erika said.

Mrs. McGillacuddy thought she saw something there beyond the hedgerow and headed toward them.

Melanie said, "She's coming this way!"

Erika was no longer concerned. "Wait. So what? It's my backyard. Nice shot, Melanie."

"Thanks."

Mrs. McGillacuddy was nearly to the hedge when her intoxicated husband slurred, "Mil-dred, sl-look who's just arrived. It's Hazel Woods, Dear."

Mrs. McGillacuddy stopped, gave the hedgerow a good long, searing look, and then snorted as she turned to join her husband. She had become distracted. She had no idea who was Hazel Woods.

THE NEWS

"Gotta go," Melanie said.

"Ditto," Jo added.

Erika bid her friends good-bye and went into the house. Mooflee followed her. She found her mom in the kitchen preparing dinner.

"Hi, Mom."

"Hi, Sweetie. How was the party?"

"Fun. Victoria and her friends tried to spoil it, but they went away."

"Mrs. M called again, Erika. She complained that Mooflee was digging in her rose garden again just before her party."

Upon hearing her name, the sheepdog sat down and perked her ears. She looked at Mrs. Reisling as if to say, "Who me?"

Mrs. Reisling continued. "We have to find some way to teach her not to go over into their yard."

Puzzled, Erika said, "I don't know why she keeps doing that, Mom. It's not like her to leave our yard. She must be going over there for something. There was a sheepdog over there today. Maybe Moof just wanted to go over there and talk." She then walked over to her dog, gave her a noogie on the head with her knuckle, and asked, "Is that what you wanted to do, Moof-ster? Go over and play with the other sheepy? Hmm?"

The big dog enjoyed Erika's noogie, hung out her tongue, and smiled as if to say, "I ain't tellin'."

Mrs. Reisling raised her eyebrow and added, "She also said that you stuck out your tongue at her when she drove by earlier today."

"Mom, she deserved it. She made an ugly face at me. She's such a mean old, grouch."

"I'm sure you're right about that, Sweetie, but she's just an old woman who's not going to change. And just because she's an old grump doesn't mean that you have to lower yourself to her level and be one, too. Does it?"

"No. I guess not, Mom. I wouldn't want people thinking I was *anything* like Mrs. McGillacuddy."

"Okay, then." Changing the subject, Mrs. Reisling asked, "How do you feel?"

Knowing her mother was referring to the effects of the morning's chemo treatment, Erika shrugged and answered, "Not bad. I felt good during the party. Keeping busy always helps me to not think about being sick; but I am beginning to feel a little queasy now. I think I'm just going to take it easy tonight."

"I think that's a good idea," Mrs. Reisling agreed. "You've been a real busy person lately; playing and biking and swimming with your friends and all." Noticing the red stains on her shirt, she asked, "What happened to your shirt?"

Erika merely said, "Oh, that. It's just pizza, that's all."

"Take it off and throw it in the laundry. Your dad will be home any moment and dinner will be ready soon, so go upstairs and clean up."

"On my way," Erika said and hurried out of the kitchen.

Mooflee stayed behind to "monitor" the kitchen floor situation in hopes that Mrs. Reisling might accidentally drop some tidbit or crumb while preparing dinner. She plopped her body down in the middle of the floor and waited.

Michele was watching television in the family room as Erika passed through the room on her way upstairs.

"*Rugrats* is on," she said. "Want to watch it with me?"

"Maybe after I change, 'Chele."

Erika had just finished putting on clean clothes when she heard her dad's car pull into the driveway.

Mr. Reisling stepped into the house and gave his wife a hug and greeted Mooflee.

"How was your day?" he asked.

"It was allll-right."

"What happened?" he asked with a knowing smile. He knew whenever his wife said "allll-right" with that long, drawn out "alll" that something had happened.

"Mooflee crossed the 'Berlin Wall' this morning and that prompted a call from the M's."

"Oh, lovely. Nice of them to call. I'm sure they had pleasant things to say to you."

"No big deal. They were having a garden party over there and were too busy to get worked up over it. They chased Mooflee home and that was that. It seems Mooflee was attracted to one of their guest's sheepdog."

"The M's actually allowed a *dog* on their property? Will wonders ever cease?" he asked with sarcasm. Mr. Reisling walked over to Mooflee, petted her on the head, and said, "What do you think of that, Moof? Real progress, huh?"

Mooflee licked Mr. Reisling's hand while thinking real progress would come the day the old witch next door took her rake and moved away.

"Although, they were more upset that Erika stuck her tongue out at Mrs. M as she was driving home," Mrs. Reisling added.

"Oh. Well, that's not so good. But she probably deserved it. I probably would have done the same," Mr. Reisling snickered as he went to the refrigerator and poured himself a glass of milk. He glanced at his wife and noticed tears were running down her face.

"What's wrong, Kathy? Surely you're not upset about that? Erika sticking her tongue out at Mrs. McGillacuddy is not *that* terrible a thing."

"Rick...Doctor Mervis called today. He thinks the leukemia has come back."

27

Mr. Reisling's mirthful expression dissolved. The playfulness dropped from his voice as he looked into his wife's red eyes. "Oh...no. Relapse?" he asked, just barely whispering the word.

Mooflee noticed the change in their conversation's tone. She looked from Mr. Reisling to Mrs. Reisling.

Mrs. Reisling nodded. "Looks that way. They need to do more tests, though."

"What about the donor?"

"They're still looking."

He sighed. "No. I was hoping this day would never come," he said quietly as he hugged his wife.

"Me, too."

"Does she know?"

"I haven't told her yet."

Mooflee rose from the kitchen floor and sauntered into the living room.

The kitchen suddenly went silent for what seemed a long time to Erika who was listening to the conversation from the other room. She had heard her father drive in and had gone downstairs to greet him. The sound of the sadness and disappointment in her parents' voices gave the little girl a chill.

Erika quietly turned around and headed for the stairs to her bedroom. Mooflee saw her and followed.

"Aren't you going to watch *Rugrats* with me?" Michele asked from the couch.

"No. Not now, Sis," she said going up the stairs.

Disappointed, Michele stepped into the kitchen. "Daddy? Mom? What's wrong with Erika?" There was sadness in her voice.

"Why, Michele?" her mom asked.

"She just went up the stairs real quiet-like. She didn't even want to watch *Rugrats* with me."

Mrs. Reisling looked at her husband with alarm.

Erika's dad knocked on her door. When there was no answer he entered and found Erika sitting at her chess table by the window. She was staring out at the McGillacuddy's house. Mooflee was sitting beside her, being petted.

"Erika?"

"Yes, Dad?"

He could tell she knew.

"I guess you heard us talking in the kitchen, huh?"

"Yes." She continued to stare at the McGillacuddy's.

Mr. Reisling sat down in the chair opposite her. "I'm sorry. We were going to tell you. Mom only just found out and was telling me."

Erika said nothing.

"It's time to eat, Erika. Let's go downstairs and have one of mom's nice dinners." When she didn't respond, Mr. Reisling asked, "What's the matter, Sweetie?"

"It's Mrs. McGillacuddy. Melanie and I were spying on her party through the hedge and one of her guests asked who were her neighbors? She said, 'Nobody important. Just some mundane couple with their bratty little child and awful dog.' It made me so mad to hear someone say nasty things like that about us."

"Erika, you just have to ignore what she says. She's an old lady who probably didn't have any friends when she was growing up. And she probably wouldn't have any friends now if it weren't for her money. Don't trouble yourself worrying about her. She's not the one who's important here."

"Dad...is there going to be a donor?"

"Sweetie, I'm sure we'll find one."

"I'm scared," she said rushing over to hug her father.

"It's okay to be scared, Erika. I'm so sorry you found out that way. We were going to tell you. Honest."

"I'm scared of leaving everyone. You and mom and 'Cheley and Mooflee will be left without me. How will you all manage? Will you all be all right?"

Mr. Reisling smiled, touched by the thought she was worried more about them than herself. "Listen, we'll be fine. And so will you. They'll find a donor. Don't worry."

"Are you sure?"

Mr. Reisling smiled. "Of course I'm sure. Don't you worry one little bit, Sweetheart."

"What about the cost of the transplant?"

"Erika, don't worry about that either. Money will be raised. Okay? You leave that to mom and me. You just have fun and enjoy your summer. That's all you have to do."

Erika whispered to herself, "It was the best of times, it was the worst of times..."

Mr. Reisling said, "Dickens."

"Very good, Dad."

"You've been in my library again, I see," he observed. He was pleased.

She nodded.

"And it's not 'the worst of times,'" he added. "It'll work out. Just like it did last winter. Listen...Doctor Mervis suggested that you go to Camp Good Days for a week."

"Where all of the 'doomed' kids go for their last year on the planet?" Erika said with bitterness. She looked down at her chess table and crossed her arms.

"Erika! We've been through that. That's not true, and you know it. Lots of kids go to Camp Good Days and not just the ones who are *really* bad off."

"You mean 'dying,'" Erika said. "It's okay to say the word, Dad."

"Sweetheart, it sounds like a wonderful place."

"Hm," she grunted.

"It really does."

She resumed petting Mooflee who continued to sit quietly beside her. Erika looked out the window again and said nothing.

"Look...your mom and I are not going to make you go if you don't want to. But there are lots of kids who do go, and they have a good time. There's swimming in the lake, fishing, cookouts, campfires, sing-alongs. All kinds of activities. They even have go-carts. It sounds like great fun. And you know what else?"

"What?" she said glumly.

"I'll bet most of those kids are just like you: they're just as scared as you are about going to camp. So, you see? You probably have something in common with them already."

"Dad, I don't know," she said.

"All I'm asking is you just try it. Give it a chance. Hey, if you don't like it, we'll come, bail you out, and bring you home. Okay?"

"Oh-kay," Erika said reluctantly after thinking about it. "I'll go. I'll probably hate it, but I'll go."

"That's my girl," Mr. Reisling said with affection as he hugged his eldest daughter again. He loved his daughter very much and knew she was only speaking with bitterness because she was scared. He knew she had every right to be.

"Can Mooflee go with me?" she asked, looking into the sheepdog's hairy face.

The big dog's ears suddenly perked.

"I don't think so, Erika. There are over a hundred kids going to the camp and if everyone brought their dog...well, they just wouldn't have the room. Besides, Sweetie, there are so many activities that you wouldn't have time to take care of Mooflee, anyway."

"I suppose," Erika said, reluctantly going along with her dad. She was obviously disappointed.

Mooflee was, too. Her ears dropped.

"Come on," Mr. Reisling said with enthusiasm. "Let's go down for dinner."

LEAVING FOR CAMP

Two weeks later, on a sunny, Saturday morning Erika gave Mooflee a big, good-bye hug. The warm, furry animal then licked her and barked. Her family then piled into the car and drove her to the Camp Good Days bus which was scheduled to leave Canandaigua at ten. The yellow bus was already in its parking spot when they arrived. The Reislings saw several other families sending their children off to the camp. A cheerful and energetic young, black woman wearing a "Camp Good Days" baseball cap and a clipboard in her hand approached them.

"Good morning! You must be the Reislings," she said.

"Yes, that's right," Mr. Reisling said.

"And you must be Erika," she said to Erika. "I'm Sandi. I'm one of the camp counselors." She extended her hand and Erika shook it.

"Hi," Erika said. She adjusted her cutesy red hat.

Sandi said, "I'm glad you could make it. You're the last one. We're just about ready to leave, so whenever you're ready just take your backpack and climb aboard the bus."

"Okay," Erika said.

Sandi smiled and winked, and then left to attend to another family.

Michele asked, "Daddy, can I go to the camp with Erika?"

"No, Sweetie. I'm sorry. You're too young."

"Phooey! I'm always too young for everything. I can't wait to be old."

"Don't worry, 'Cheley. You'll be old enough soon," Mr. Reisling said, realizing Michele was sad that her sister was leaving. "I'll tell you what, though. Suppose I take you and one of your friends to the movies and the arcade. Would you like that instead?"

"Yeah!" Michele answered with delight. She looked at her sister and then - in a sing-song manner - sang, "Erika, have fun at that caa-amp. I'm going to the mooo-vies."

Just then Erika saw Victoria and her mother drive by in their car, on their way to shop, she guessed. As they drove by, she saw Victoria shake her head spastically and stick her tongue out at her through the window. Erika merely frowned at her childish gesture.

Mrs. Reisling, not noticing Victoria and her mom, said reassuringly, "Erika, you'll have fun. Really. You'll meet a lot of interesting kids there."

Erika looked doubtful.

Her father added, "Trust us. Okay?"

"I do," Erika said, finally relenting. She didn't want to go, but, there was something, a tiny, nagging part of her that told her she *should* go.

"Good. We'll see you right here in a week, Kiddo. And remember our promise - we'll come and get you, if you really want us to," Mr. Reisling said as he hugged his eldest daughter good-bye. "But I know you'll make lots of new friends."

"I'll try."

"That's my girl," he said and hugged her again.

Mrs. Reisling then hugged her daughter and said, "I know you'll have fun, Darling. I love you."

"I love you, too, Mom."

"You call us if you have any problems. Okay?" she said.

"Okay, Mom," Erika replied.

"Bye, Erika," Michele said as she waved to her big sister.

"Bye, 'Chele. You take good care of Mooflee. Make sure she stays out of trouble."

"I will."

"Bye," Erika said, reluctantly waving to her family as she climbed aboard the bus.

As Erika boarded the bus she saw there were nearly two-dozen children and two other counselors besides Sandi. Some of the children had crutches. Some had leg braces. One boy had a patch over an eye. Many had no hair like herself, although not all. Many wore headbands. Most had a warm sparkle in their eyes. The excitement of going to camp tingled in the air and Erika could sense it. She felt a sudden surge of relief pass through her as she realized there was nothing unusual or alien about this group of kids. A few children were gazing out the windows, but most were talking and laughing. Erika found an empty seat by a window and was about to sit down when one peppy little girl called to her.

"Hey, why don't you sit over here?" she asked pointing to the seat next to her.

Erika looked at the vibrant girl - who was nearly her own age - and could not refuse. She looked like she might be a fun person. Erika walked over to her and sat down beside her.

Counselor Sandi was the last person to board the bus and as soon as she did, the door closed and the journey began.

The vehicle rumbled away down the street. Mr. and Mrs. Reisling waved as it departed. Mrs. Reisling's eyes swelled with tears as they watched the bus disappear down the road.

"She'll be back in a week," Mr. Reisling reminded her as he gave his wife a hug.

Mrs. Reisling nodded. "I know," she said, wiping the tears from her eyes.

"Can we go to the movies, now?" Michele asked, ready to move on to the next order of the day's business.

Both parents smiled.

"Yes, let's go," Mr. Reisling said, excitement in his voice. "If we hurry we can catch the matinee."

"Goody!"

MAKING FRIENDS AT CAMP GOOD DAYS

"I'm Yancy Cromwell," the bubbly, brown-eyed girl announced proudly after Erika had sat down.

Yancy Cromwell had long, rusty red, slightly wavy hair and a warm and cheerful personality. She was extremely outgoing and was overflowing with energy.

"I'm Erika Reisling. Nice to meet you, Yancy."

"It's nice to meet you, Erika. Are you excited about going to camp this year?" she asked. It certainly was clear that *she* was excited.

"This is my first time."

"Ah! I thought so! Well, let me tell you something about camp," Yancy said. She then paused for what seemed like a long, long time.

"What?" Erika finally asked.

"It's great!" she declared. "It's the world's neatest place!"

"You aren't kiddin', Yancy," said a flaming red-haired boy who slipped into the seat behind them. "I'm Marvin Tinkel. I like movie nights the best!"

"I'm Erika," she said to the freckle-faced youngster. She noticed he wore leg braces.

"Yeah, I know. I heard. They do movie nights outside under the stars and meteors," Marvin continued. Marvin was full of enthusiasm, too.

"Marvin's a science fiction freak," Yancy explained.

"Yeah! My favorite is 'The Day the Earth Stood Still.' I love science fiction," he said.

"*You're* science fiction, Marvin," said a little girl seated on the other side of the bus. "What planet are *you* from?"

Marvin then stood up, snapped to attention, and clicked his leg braces together making a clunky metallic sound. His face became zombie-like, his eyes locked forward, and he uttered in a robotic voice, "I am Gort. What's the secret password?"

"Not another summer of this stuff!" Yancy protested. She looked at Erika and said, "He's playing a character from the movie. To get him to stop, tell him 'Klatu berada nickto.' That'll snap him out of it. I guess. I hope!"

Erika repeated the phrase to Marvin and the young boy clicked his leg braces together again and instantly snapped out of his Gort impersonation.

Two young women in their twenties approached the children.

"Hi Erika. I'm Marina, and this is Stency. We're your camp counselors."

"Hi," Erika said.

"First time going to Camp Good Days, huh?"

"Yes."

"Well, it's a great place where you can do as much as you want and meet as many kids as you'd like. If you have any problems or questions don't be afraid to come to us or ask any of the other counselors. We're there to help you have a fun time."

"Fun time?" Yancy asked. "You're going to have a *fantastic* time!"

"Thank you," Erika said to both Marina and Stency.

The bus cruised over the hilly, country roads between Canandaigua and the little town of Branchport, the home of the camp. Along the road they passed Canandaigua Lake and countless cottages crowding its shores. They passed old farmhouses and falling down barns. There were vineyards and cows. Cornfields and self-service roadside vegetable stands. Farm tractors and hay wagons. The occasional abandoned car buried by tall weeds. More vineyards. Green fields. They were in the heart of winemaking country in the Finger Lakes. It was a bright sunny day. Sky blue. Not a cloud to be seen.

As the bus rolled on, the kids talked and laughed. It was Erika's first contact with other children who, like herself, were dealing with a relentless and unseen enemy from within. Something that was not their fault and yet was placing their lives in grave danger. The kids were just like her. Normal, average kids. Her earlier fears of being on a bus with so many sick kids - the "doomed kids" as she had put it - like herself began melting away. The crutches, the braces, the patches, the scarves and hats were all quickly forgotten. Some of the kids actually did look ill, but she could see clearly that they were happy. Erika knew she was lucky to be healthy again. She knew she was lucky she could ride her bicycle and shoot squirt guns at her friends. She knew she was lucky she could still go to the park and go swimming and throw Frisbees with her friends. Many of the kids couldn't do those things. As the bus journeyed on, Erika began to feel at ease being there for she knew she had a lot in common with these kids. After all, it had only been last winter that she had undergone massive chemotherapy treatments. It had only been last winter that she had been totally incapable of doing anything, much less ride a bicycle or a bus to a camp.

Counselor Patrick, a tall lanky fellow with a good-natured face and thirty years of life under his belt, was sitting at a picnic table filling in an activity sheet with campers' names when he heard the sound of an engine coming. He looked up from his sheet and spotted the yellow bus coming down the road.

He instantly jumped up and leaped over the table. He began yelling, "Hey! Everybody! Hey! Here comes the last bus!! Here comes the last bus!!" Excitement and jubilation filled his voice. "Come on! Calling all hands! Calling all hands! Hurry everyone!"

When the bus turned into the camp's parking lot, the arrival was more than Erika had expected. Camp counselors, balloon-bearing clowns, and children poured out of the buildings and activity areas and ran from all directions to greet the bus. Those who couldn't run, walked. Those who couldn't walk were wheeled. Those who couldn't be wheeled were carried. All of these people, children and adults, were all happily yelling and shouting, cheering and clapping, completely ecstatic over the new arrivals. As Erika and the other kids climbed off the bus, they quickly became absorbed into this happy mass of warm-hearted human beings. Erika was astounded by the warm reception and her worries disappeared. Most everyone that surrounded her suddenly seemed like they were part of one, big happy family.

As the happy receptionists gradually dispersed, the counselors showed the new arrivals to their cabins. Marina led Erika and Yancy to theirs. Erika was happy to see that Yancy was assigned to her cabin. Entering the small wooden structure which had the number "6" over the door, Erika found she was one of five girls to be bunking there. The beds were set up three on one side of the room and two on the other. Erika set her backpack down on one of the empty beds and then introduced herself to her roommates. The other girls in cabin six were Barnetta, Tully, and Evy. Erika learned that Yancy was from Naples, which was near her hometown of Canandaigua. Tully had come all the way from Boston. This surprised Erika that someone would travel such a great distance to be at the camp. Evy was from Rochester, and Barnetta was from Syracuse.

She wondered briefly what everyone's problem was. Barnetta was the quiet one of the group. She looked very pale and weak, but smiled a lot and was pleasant. She wore red glasses and a cute black fedora with an ace of hearts card stuffed in the hatband. In her arms, she held an adorable stuffed bunny rabbit. She said she liked to read and swim. Tully's left forearm was missing. She said she had come to the camp to meet new kids and spoke of her love to play tennis. Evy wore a silk batik scarf. It was neatly wrapped around and knotted behind her head. She said she liked to draw pictures of people and that she was going to be an artist. She had brought her sketchbook and drawing pencils. Erika knew her own hairless head told them briefly of her story. Yancy, on the other hand, was a puzzle. She didn't seem to be suffering from anything other than a big overabundance of energy. Erika's curiosity passed. It really didn't matter. Camp time was supposed to be vacation time from those troubles.

After the brief introductions and pleasantries were exchanged, the girls heard a bell ringing and then someone calling from outside. Erika didn't hear what was said, but Yancy did as she perked her ears.

"Come on!" she shouted and then darted for the screen door. "The counselors want us outside. Time to play, girls!"

Without taking time to unpack, all of the girls followed Yancy and were quickly out the door. Sketchbooks and stuffed rabbits were left behind. There would be plenty of time to unpack later. Camp time had truly begun!

There were over one-hundred and fifty children of all ages at the camp that week. The camp was nestled on Keuka Lake's west side and was well equipped. There were recreation rooms which housed, among other things, Ping-Pong, billiard tables, video games, and television-VCRs. There were assorted activity buildings which resembled small cabins where kids could try their skills at handicrafts, paint pictures, make music, or go online with a computer and send email to friends and family. There were plenty of sports facilities, including basketball and tennis courts, and a sand-filled volley ball court. There were swing sets, a jungle gym, canoes, a miniature golf course, a small petting zoo, and a go-cart track. There was a costume barn for those who wanted to perform skits. There was even an Outward Bound-style rope and rock climbing obstacle course. There was a small beach for swimming as well as a dock from which to fish.

There were over twenty-five glowing and enthusiastic counselors and assistants to help the children. The children were divided into different activity groups based on their ages, abilities, and the children's own preferences. Each group's counselor then led their charges off to the different activity areas. Marina was the counselor for Erika's group and she organized a volleyball game right away. Three of Erika's roommates were on her team, including Tully. Despite the loss of a forearm, Tully was an aggressive player; a result of her abilities on the tennis court. Barnetta watched with enthusiasm from the bench. Her weakened condition prevented her from playing volleyball with her cabin mates; however, she was a good cheerleader and provided encouragement. As the game went on Erika got to know all of the children on her team as well as those on the other team. She felt very warm and excited by this place and all of her previous fears seemed to completely disappear into the clean lake air.

After playing awhile, Erika noticed a lonely-looking boy sitting at a chess table beside the lake not far from where they were playing volleyball. Like many of the children, he wore a scarf on his head. He was playing chess by himself.

"Who is that boy over there wearing the purple scarf?" she asked Yancy.

"That's Luc," Yancy said. "He likes to be by himself when he comes to camp."

"He's been here before?"

"He's been here for the last two summers."

"Why does he come back?" Erika asked.

"Why not?" Yancy asked, puzzled why anyone would ask such a silly question.

Erika noticed that Luc continued to study the chessboard and seemed oblivious to volleyball or anything else around him.

After the game, Counselor Marina suggested a swim time for anyone interested before the meal hour commenced. Everyone was interested! Erika and the others went back to their cabins and changed into their swimsuits. It was still a bright, sunny day and the children jumped into the lovely clear lake. There they frolicked and splashed each other. Some used the time to build sand castles on the beach.

Later, one of the campers was assigned the job of ringing the old ship's bell for dinner. Dinner was served alongside the lake beneath the large picnic pavilion. Dinner that night consisted of everyone's favorite: salad, hamburgers, and French fries. For dessert, there were "Counselor Patrick's Mega-Monster Sundaes!" Prepared exclusively by Counselor Patrick and his helpers, this delight consisted of five different types of ice cream which were topped with three types of nuts, chocolate and vanilla chips, M&Ms, and smothered with thick hot fudge and butterscotch. Counselor Patrick pretended to be a mad, "Frankensteinian" scientist for the kids as he and his helpers prepared sundaes for each child, treating each dessert as though it were a new and unique creation, which, individually, they were.

As Erika ate her "Monster Sundae" with her roommates, she saw Luc again, the scarf-wearing boy who had been playing chess by himself beside the lake. He was having his Monster Sundae at the end of the next table over. Across from him was seated a young woman with medium-length, black hair and brown eyes. The woman was talking to him. Erika still wondered why he kept to himself.

At sunset, the American flag was taken down by one of the counselors and the children, tired, went to bed early. It had been a long day and most had come from long distances. It was now time for rest.

"Is everybody okay?" Counselor Marina asked as she looked in on the girls in Erika's cabin.

All of them answered with a big, happy "Yes!"

"Okay then," Marina said. "Welcome to Camp Good Days. I'm glad all of you could come. I'm so happy to meet you all."

"Thank you," the girls responded. "You, too."

"My cabin is right next door if you need me," Marina said. "Good night, and I'll see you tomorrow."

"Good night, Marina," Erika and Yancy said.

"Oh, and girls..." Marina paused as she began to leave. "No pillow fights. Okay? Go to sleep and save your energies for tomorrow."

"Okay, Marina," the girls answered.

"Good night then. Pleasant dreams," the counselor said. She then left.

No sooner had Marina closed the door behind her when all five girls began slamming each other with their pillows.

Outside, Marina laughed to herself. She knew it was going to be a fun week at camp.

A NEW FRIEND

The next day was as sunny and pretty as the first day. The sun rose over the green hills directly across the lake and at 6:45 the counselors ran from cabin to cabin banging and clanging pots and pans against cabin doors, waking the campers. Erika and her roommates dragged themselves out of bed and then showered and dressed.

At 7:45 everyone in the camp, but one, gathered by the flagpole for colors.

"Where's Danny Stigwood?" Counselor Patrick wanted to know, glancing at his clipboard. "He's the only one missing."

A group of Danny's cabin mates indicated that Danny had refused to get out of bed.

"Oh? Is that so?" Patrick questioned. "We'll just see about this."

Patrick, two other counselors, and one of the camp's volunteer doctors marched off to Danny's cabin, leaving one hundred and forty-nine campers waiting by the flagpole. A few minutes later - after determining that Danny was basically okay - they all emerged from Danny's cabin carrying Danny's bed - with Danny in it. They returned to the flagpole and set the bed down in front of everyone. All of the campers erupted with laughter and a red-faced Danny Stigwood hid his face beneath his outdoor bed covers.

Now everyone was present and the flag ceremony began. Immediately afterwards the ship's bell was rung, signaling that breakfast was being served in the roomy Union Hall. Danny leapt from his bed and raced back to his cabin to get dressed. He was nicknamed "Danny Flagpole" for the rest of the week.

With so many activities to choose from, the children made their choices for the day after breakfast and were then divided up into groups. Erika and Yancy spent the early part of the morning on the dock fishing while her roommates went off to other activities. Tully headed off with a small group to play tennis. Barnetta went with another group to the petting zoo to help feed and brush the animals. Evy hurried off to the Art Shed to see what neat things happened there.

Erika's fishing efforts were not successful. She had a few nibbles and provided a few fish with some juicy worms, but she didn't catch anything. Yancy, on the other hand, caught a medium-sized trout and was ecstatic. She presented it to Phil, the counselor who was supervising their fishing activity. Counselor Phil congratulated her on a fine catch and then gently unhooked the trout and placed it back in the lake.

As Erika and Yancy headed for their next activity, they heard the sound of engines. They looked in the direction of the go-cart track and saw little Marvin Tinkel, Danny Flagpole, and other boys and girls whipping around the track in their go-carts. Marvin was having the time of his life.

Laughter from above suddenly prompted both girls to look skyward.

In the rope climb area, adjacent to the go-cart track, Erika saw a girl her own age hopping along the length of a long, airborne pole. The elevated pole was suspended on both ends by two, tall telephone poles. She was wearing a harness and was attached to a safety line. She was in no danger of falling. However, what made the sight so remarkable to both Erika and Yancy was the girl had only one leg.

"She must be thirty feet above the ground!" Erika said with amazement as she watched.

"I'm on top of the world!" the tethered, young girl shouted to the sky as she made her way across the pole, hopping all the way.

A round of clapping arose from the counselors and campers who were on the ground providing support and supervision.

"Way to go, Gloria!" one of the campers shouted up to her.

"Wow!" Erika said. "I'd be frightened to do that with *two* legs."

"Not me," Yancy said. "I did it last year. It's a blast! You get hoisted up like Peter Pan and then off you go! You should try it."

"Maybe I will," Erika said with caution.

"Oh, I've got to stop by the Infirmary for my pills," Yancy remembered. "I'll meet up with you at the Baking Shed."

"All right," Erika said as she watched her go. She then noticed her cabin mate Evy sitting on a log nearby. She had her sketchbook on her lap and was drawing. Erika wandered over to see what she was creating.

"Hi, Evy."

Evy looked up and smiled. "Hi, Erika. How was fishing?"

"Okay. I didn't catch anything, but it was fun. Yancy caught a trout, but we threw it back. Do you mind if I have a look?"

"No, I don't mind. I'm just practicing my sketching."

Erika looked with amazement at the girl's work. On the single sheet were several small sketches. The sketch she was working on at that moment depicted the campers in the rope climb area, including the one-legged girl called Gloria they had just seen hop across the thirty-foot tall pole. There was a sketch of "Freddie the Clown" standing on his head on a tricycle. Another small sketch showed, what was no doubt, their cabin mate Tully hitting a ball on the tennis court.

"This is really good work, Evy," Erika praised. "You're very talented."

"Thanks," Evy said with modesty. "They're okay." She took a moment to adjust the light blue, silk batik scarf on her head. "When I go home I'm going to redraw and paint some of these and call them my 'Camp Good Days Series.'"

"That's a neat idea, Evy."

Erika noticed another drawing on the same sheet, but did not recognize the scene. It showed a boy sitting on a park bench beneath a towering statue made of balloons.

She pointed to it and asked, "Where was this one drawn?"

"Oh, that's right over there, beside the Infirmary," Evy said, nodding to the right.

Erika turned in the direction of the Infirmary and, sure enough, there was the very scene Evy had drawn. The boy in the sketch was still there, sitting on a park bench beneath a tall bronze statue. Erika realized he was the boy called Luc. She decided to walk over and say hello.

Approaching the boy, Erika said, "Hello. We're going to the Baking Shed. Would you like to bake with us?"

Luc looked around to see who Erika was talking to. Realizing she was addressing him, he replied curtly, "Me? Bake? I don't bake." He spoke with a slight accent.

"Well, you don't have to be that way about it," Erika said.

"Hey, do you see this statue and these benches?" the boy asked, annoyance in his voice.

Erika looked at the attractive, ten-foot tall, bronze creation. It was situated in the middle of a circle of four park benches. It depicted three hands holding three balloons by their strings; hands and balloons reaching high for the sky. It seemed to symbolize fun, and hope.

"Yes?" she answered.

"*This* area is considered a *quiet* area. That means you don't *talk* to anybody who is sitting here."

"Oh," she said, a little embarrassed. "I-I'm sorry. I didn't know."

The boy then retreated back to his thoughts and completely ignored her. Erika retreated a few steps backwards, quietly turned around, and headed for the Bake Shed.

During their hour of baking, Erika and her campmates made peanut butter cookies and chocolate chip cookies. Once made, they then promptly devoured them. It was a popular activity. Afterwards, she and Yancy went canoeing. They stayed close to the shoreline so they could look over the side and look for neat things on the stony bottom of the clear lake. The entire time they were under the watchful eye of a camp counselor very near by. In the afternoon, Marina organized another volleyball game and Erika and her cabin mates played. Again, Barnetta watched from the sidelines.

It was a good game with some incredibly long rallies. At one point during the game the volleyball was knocked out of bounds and Erika chased after it. It rolled toward the lake and came to a stop only a few feet from the chess table. At the chess table sat Luc. He was twirling the queen. Erika picked up the ball and threw it to the others.

"You'll never get into heaven with a throw like that," he quipped, speaking with his slight accent.

Erika stopped and asked, "Oh? What do you know about heaven?"

"Well," the boy said as he twiddled with the queen and then spun it around again, "I know that bad volleyball players can't play on the team up there."

"Then I guess I won't be playing on the team. But I'm still going. *If* I have to go."

He looked up from the twirling chess piece and looked her straight in the eye. "*I'm* going," he stated firmly as though nothing would get in his way.

His tone startled Erika and she gave him a long, hard look.

Some of the kids from her group called out to her. "Come on, Erika. Let's play." "Erika!" Yancy called out. "Come back!"

Erika turned and yelled back to them. "I don't want to play any more."

Counselor Marina looked at her with encouragement and asked, "Are you sure?"

"Yes. Thanks."

Hopeful Erika would change her mind, Marina watched a moment more, but then noticed something else was happening. Luc and Erika were actually talking. The counselor smiled to herself. Luc rarely spoke to anybody.

Marina called out to the others, "Okay...everyone, rotate. Jimmy it's your turn to serve."

"I'm Erika Reisling. What's your name?"

"Luc Maille. Nice to meet you."

"I'm sorry I disturbed you earlier at the Statue area. I didn't know it was kind of a sacred place."

"That's okay. I'm not angry, but I still don't bake."

"Where are you from?"

"Paris."

"Paris? Why so far away?"

"I am waiting, with my mom, for treatment at John Hopkins." Luc looked toward the main lodge and nodded. "That's her over there."

Erika turned to see. A young woman in her thirties with medium length black hair appeared in the lodge door. It was the same woman Erika had seen the night before eating with Luc. She seemed nervous as she chewed a fingernail, pushed her hair back, and surveyed the camp. When she sighted her son, she seemed relieved and then headed for him.

"She's a little high-strung," he added.

"What's wrong with you?" Erika asked.

"Brain tumor," he answered with a shrug as though it were no big deal. He might as well have said he had an ingrown toenail. "It's as big as a Ping-Pong ball they tell me."

"I'm sorry to hear it," Erika said.

"There's nothing to be sorry about. It's not your fault. It's not even *my* fault. What's wrong with you?"

"Leukemia. I need a bone marrow transplant."

"I've heard about those," Luc said, matter-of-factly. "Sometimes people get one. Sometimes they don't." He shrugged again and then asked, "Are you getting one?"

"I don't know," Erika answered. She found herself uncomfortable talking about it. She never liked to talk about it, especially after last winter when she was in the hospital being treated. "Depends if they can find a donor."

"Hmm," he nodded to himself. "So, are you scared?"

"Of what?" Erika asked.

"Of dying? What else?"

"I don't think about it."

"You don't think about it? That's a lie," Luc said.

"It is not."

"Everybody thinks about it."

"Well, I don't, so quit pestering me about it."

"You can't get into heaven if you're a liar, you know."

"I don't lie so I *am* getting into heaven."

"See? So you do think about it."

"That's not what I meant. I *don't* think about it. You're mixing up words and being nothing more than a pest," she snapped as she became frustrated. "How foolish of me to think you might be a nice person. I'm going back to play volleyball."

She turned to leave.

"Hey, wait. Don't go," he said.

Erika stopped and turned around. "Why shouldn't I?"

"I am a nice person. I'm not a pest. I just believe in telling the truth, that's all."

No longer angry with him, Erika approached the chess table.

"So, do you sit here all of the time and play chess by yourself?"

"No. Not all of the time." Suddenly, Luc was overtaken with an idea. "I know...speaking of Ping-Pong balls, do you want to play?"

Erika shook her head in confusion. "Ping-Pong? Who said anything about Ping-Pong?"

"I did. I said I had a brain tumor as big as a Ping-Pong ball. Don't you remember?"

"Oh, yes. I do remember that. Where is it?"

"In my head!"

"No! The Ping-Pong table??"

"Ohhhh...thaaat. Follow me."

Luc made one last move on the chessboard and then stood up.

"Who's winning your chess game," Erika asked as she followed.

"I am, of course!"

Luc's mother called out as she approached. "Luc! Luc! Te voila!"

"Ouai, Maman," Luc replied with indifference.

Mrs. Maille warned, "Tu ne dois pas t'exposer au soleil toute la journee sans creme anti-solaire."

"It's okay, Maman. Pas de probleme. I'm fine. I don't need sunscreen." To Erika he said, "She always makes such a fuss." To his mom, "Maman, this is Erika. Voici Erika."

"Hello," Mrs. Maille said.

"Hello," Erika responded.

"She doesn't understand much English," he explained. "I'm trying to help her learn." To his mom, Luc said, "We're going inside. On va a l'interieur."

Luc led the way and left his mother behind. She watched helplessly as the two children walked away. They went to the recreation center where the Ping-Pong tables were located. Mrs. Maille then turned around and faced the lake, not quite sure what to do.

Counselor Marina, still playing volleyball with her group, glanced over and watched the two children go. She was pleased to see Luc had found someone he would talk to.

The recreation center was a hub of activity. There were many children of assorted ages playing. Some were in wheelchairs, chatting about boyfriends and girlfriends. Others were talking about computers and the latest video games, while some actually were playing video games in the game section of the room. Others were playing board games. Some kids were playing billiards, including a girl who was deep in concentration, studying the angle of her stick, as she prepared to make her shot. Erika noticed the girl had lost a leg and then realized it was Gloria, the girl she had seen hopping across the thirty-foot high, elevated pole that morning in the rope area. Erika then saw a boy younger than herself aggressively playing Ping-Pong. The young boy, who was missing an arm, was beating the pants off his opponent who struggled in vain to return his powerful shots. Many of the kids wore wildly colorful scarves or funky hats like her own. All of the kids were laughing and having fun. Erika felt right at home.

Erika and Luc found an unused Ping-Pong table and played for a while. They talked about their friends and dogs. She told him all about Mooflee.

"You're lucky you have a dog like that," Luc said. "Mooflee sounds like a lot of fun. I bet she's all big and furry, too. Like a walking pillow."

"Yes, she is. Plus, she's smart. She knows everything."

"My Airedale is like that. I play with her all of the time when I'm home. I do miss her," Luc said.

"Why don't you like to play with the other kids?" Erika asked him.

He shrugged. "Most of my friends from last summer aren't here. So why make a bunch of new friends if you're not going to see them again?"

"Why come to camp at all if you're not going to play with anyone?"

"I'm playing with you," he said. "But I don't mind sitting alone at times, either. Sometimes I'm my own best company. You should try it."

Erika slammed the ball, rocketing it to his side of the table. It bounced hard and fast and he missed. "There! Got ya!" Erika proclaimed.

A girl seated behind him caught the ball in between her teeth. She dropped it into her hand and tossed it to Luc.

"Good catch," Erika said to the girl, who smiled. Erika then said to Luc, "I have. I'd rather be playing."

"'You have what?" Luc asked.

"Sat alone in my room. I'd rather be playing with my friends."

She served and they began a new rally.

"What do you think about in your room?"

"Nothing much," she said.

"You do so. I bet you think about your life."

"I don't want to talk about it."

"You're scared."

Erika slammed the ball hard again and he missed again. So did the girl behind them as she tried to catch it with her teeth again.

"I am not," Erika said. "I don't want to talk about it, that's all." Erika served the ball again. Luc returned the serve and they rallied.

Luc was insistent. "You are scared."

Erika put down her paddle and let Luc's return shot bounce off into the wall.

"You're no fun, Luc. All you like to talk about is dying and I don't want to talk about that! No wonder no one plays with you," she said, unintentionally raising her voice.

Other children in the room stopped what they were doing and looked in their direction. Erika was suddenly embarrassed as the room went silent for what seemed like an eternity. Luc, realizing her embarrassment, broke the silence.

"My serve," he announced as he picked up another Ping-Pong ball. The other kids in the room resumed their talking.

Luc then replied softly, "No, I don't, Erika. I just know you're scared. I know what it's like because I *used* to be scared, too. All I'm saying is it's okay to be scared." Luc glanced down at her paddle and repeated, "It's my serve."

She picked up her paddle and the two finished the game with Erika winning.

45

Later, as they walked amongst the cabins, they talked.

"What do you mean you 'used to be scared'?" Erika asked. "You're not now?"

"No," Luc answered. "I'm sad. But I'm not scared."

She looked at him with uncertainty. "Why not?"

"Because there's nothing they can do for me."

"Really?" Erika asked. "Nothing at all?"

Luc shrugged. "They're trying, but I know they can't. So there's nothing more to worry about. There's nothing I can do about it. So, I'm not frightened anymore."

Erika thought about what Luc said. It made some sense.

They were interrupted just then as Marvin and Danny Flagpole hurried by them. The two boys were walking in a clumsy manner with their legs locked straight and their arms stiff.

"What are you doing, Marvin?" Erika asked.

Marvin looked at Erika, his head turning slowly as though it were on top of a gear-downed drive shaft. He replied in a monotonal voice, "Danny Flagpole and I are pretending to be robots from Andromeda. We are on a mission to study the lake."

"Yes," Danny added in his monotonal voice, "It is full of water and fish. We must investigate and report to our superiors."

A moment later the boys broke out in laughter and were gone.

"I've got an idea," Erika said to Luc, after a moment. She looked over at the volleyball court. It was empty. "Come with me."

Erika's roommates had finished playing and she headed for her cabin. When she and Luc arrived, they could hear the girls rushing around inside. Just then Yancy, Evy, and Tully, followed by Barnetta came through the door. They were dressed in their swimsuits.

"Erika! There you are," Yancy said excitedly. "Get your swimsuit on and join us."

"Yes, come on!" Barnetta added as she trailed behind the others.

"I'll be right there." To Luc, Erika said, "Go get your suit on and play with us."

"I don't know," he shilly-shallied. "Mama won't like it."

"What's wrong? You *scared*?" Erika teased.

"No! I'm *not* scared," he said firmly.

"Come on, then! It'll be fun!"

"All right," he agreed.

"Hurry then!" Erika said, and she dashed inside to change.

Luc rushed off to his cabin to do the same.

Later he showed up on the beach. Erika was delighted he hadn't changed his mind and retreated to the solitude of the chess table. She introduced him to her friends and they welcomed him into their Frisbee circle where he had a great time chasing the plastic saucer.

Mrs. Maille appeared soon after and was stunned to see her son in a swimsuit.

"Luc!" she called as she marched over to him. "Luc!"

"Hi, Maman," he said as he burst out laughing and caught the Frisbee.

"Luc! You catch cold," she said, struggling with her English. She resorted to French. "Tu attraperas un rhume. Il faut te secher et mettre des vetements. Tout de suite! Maintenant! Now!"

Counselors Marina and Stency were standing close by watching.

"Oh, no," Marina shook her head as she commented to Stency. "She needs to leave him alone."

"We need to talk to her," Stency said.

"I've tried, but it's no use," Marina said, shaking her head.

"Maintenant!" Mrs. Maille repeated.

Luc said to his mother, "No, Maman, I'm okay. This is fun. C'est amusant! Don't worry, Mama. Here...catch. Attrape!" Luc threw the Frisbee at his mother.

His mother - in a reflexive move that even took her by surprise - caught the disk with both hands. She looked at the plastic disk in her hand and held it up. Everyone in the circle cheered and clapped.

Mrs. Maille smiled.

Luc said proudly, "Bonne attrappe, Maman."

As worried as she was about her son, Mrs. Maille tossed the Frisbee back to Luc. She then found herself enjoying the game.

When Mrs. Maille caught it again, she laughed with joy.

"Tres bien, Maman!" Luc said.

Yancy then said to her, "Good job, Mama."

"Yes, tres bien, Mama," Erika repeated.

Before the game was over everyone was calling Mrs. Maille "Mama." Mrs. Maille was having so much fun she didn't seem to mind.

That evening Luc didn't eat alone with his mother. He ate, instead, with Erika, her roommates, and the other children. Mrs. Maille had dinner with Marina, Patrick, and Stency. Later, Luc joined them and the other kids around the campfire for stories, sing-alongs, and s'mores. It had been a good day for Luc. Thanks to Erika, he had made some new friends. Erika was pleased with herself.

PATRICK THE HERO!

The last of the s'mores were consumed and the campfire's bright flames dwindled to a mere red glow. The counselors put the happy campers to bed and wished them all a good night. A short time after lights out, Erika and her roommates dozed off to sleep.

But then, later, a small scratching sound woke them up. One by one, their eyelids opened. As they became aware that they were all awake, Erika groggily asked in the dark, "What is that?"

The girls listened. It was coming from above, up in the A-frames that supported the small cabin's wooden ceiling.

"Sounds like there's something on the roof," Yancy said.

They listened some more.

Scraatch. Scraatch.

"It sounds like it's *inside* the cabin," Barnetta said, cuddling her stuffed rabbit.

"Inside?" Tully asked, a noticeable trembling in her voice.

Yancy reached over to her night table and found her flashlight. She clicked it on and pointed it up at the ceiling. At first they didn't see anything. They heard the noise again and Yancy swung the light's beam in the direction of the sound.

"What's that dark spot in the corner," Evy asked when the light stopped on a motionless black shape.

Suddenly the dark spot moved slowly and stopped. Then the girls, all at once, saw two tiny eyes reflect in the light beam.

"What is that?" Barnetta asked. She was scared.

"It's a bat," Erika announced.

"A bat??" Tully shrieked.

The girls jumped out of bed and fled through the cabin door, screaming bloody murder into the previously quiet night. Their screaming woke up everyone in the camp. Counselor Patrick was there in an instant with a flashlight in hand.

"What's the matter?" he asked. He stood there dressed in a disheveled T-shirt and a quickly thrown-on pair of blue jeans. His feet were bare.

"There's a bat in there!" Yancy exclaimed.

"I think he bit my neck!" Barnetta cried.

"Oh, no!" Patrick responded with concern.

"I don't think he had time to bite you, Barnetta," Erika said, comforting her.

Counselor Marina arrived just then.

"What's the matter?" she asked.

"There's a bat in our cabin!" Yancy exclaimed again.

"I'll take care of it," Patrick said heading for the door. He added, "Barnetta said it bit her."

"Oh! Let's see. Where did it bite you, Sweetie?" Marina asked.

"Some place on my neck, I think," Barnetta whined.

Patrick entered the cabin with his flashlight in hand.

The children waited and listened. It seemed like Patrick was in there forever. They could see the beam from his flashlight moving around the room through the windows as he searched for the bat.

Just then the light went out.

"What happened to his light?" Tully asked.

"Patrick?" Marina called.

"Oh, no. The bat ate him!" Barnetta moaned.

"Bats don't eat people, Barnetta," Erika said. She then called to the cabin, "Patrick?"

Marina called, too. "Patrick??"

Just then there was a scream! It was Patrick. He screamed and yelled. He bumped and crashed into things inside the tiny cabin. There was a loud, resounding thud as he fell to the wooden floor. They girls could hear him rolling around and struggling and making deep grunting and gagging noises!

"Maybe we should get help for him!" Yancy said.

"Yeah. I'll go for Stency!" Tully said, turning to leave.

Just then the cabin was silent. Tully stopped. The girls took a small step toward the door.

The door flew open suddenly and Patrick jumped out onto the ground. The girls were startled.

"It was a tough battle and he put up a good fight, but I finally got him," he said proudly as he approached them.

"He wasn't *that* big," Erika said with suspicion.

"Yeah," Yancy agreed. "He was just a little thing."

"Yes, I know. He wasn't that big," Patrick said. He then raised his hand high above his head and held up the little creature. It was still alive.

The girls shrieked and jumped away.

"Wait, Girls. I was just kidding in there."

"Patrick!" Marina said, annoyed. "You had me fooled, too."

"What a rotten trick!" Yancy said.

"Boy, Patrick!" Barnetta said, admonishing the counselor.

"I know. It was a lousy prank, but look," Patrick said as he held up the bat for them to see. "He's really harmless."

"No!" the girls shouted at the same time.

Marina said, "Patrick, get rid of that thing, please."

"Okay," Patrick said reluctantly, and then he threw the bat high into the night air. "Good-bye, my warm and furry friend," he added as they as all watched the creature disappear into the dark.

The girls returned to their beds, and to the peaceful world of sleep.

THE PRANK!

The camp awoke the next morning to another bright and sunny day. Camp Good Days always held pleasant surprises of some sort every day for someone. Today was no exception. Movie night posters were tacked up in all of the public places and on trees. In addition, there was a new member on the counseling staff.

"Good morning, Batman."

"Hello, Mr. Batman."

"Hey, Batman. Where's Robin? Hee-hee."

The girls in Erika's cabin had started it, but by the end of the morning everyone at camp was calling Counselor Patrick "Batman."

"Nice shorts, Batman."

"Where'd ya get those glasses, Batman?"

"Hey, Batman! What's the movie tonight?"

A group of kids had even taken time to draw a bunch of pictures of Patrick wearing a black mask and cape and had tacked them to several trees around the camp. Patrick took the joking all in good fun.

While the jovial counselor enjoyed his new name and fame, it was improv day for Erika. She had signed up for the improvisation class along with a dozen others. The class was supposed to come up with its own skit and then perform it that night just before the movie beneath the stars. Despite his saying "no" many times, Erika managed to talk Luc into attending the class, too.

"Hey, look," sci-fi enthusiast Marvin pointed out on their way to class. "Tonight's movie night. They're showing *Plan 9 from Outer Space*!"

"So what?" Luc asked.

"It's the world's greatest movie! That's what!" Marvin announced.

The class gathered by the lake with Counselor Stency who told them they could do anything they liked as long as they worked together. After a lot of ideas were thrown out, the children decided to do a spoof on Gilligan's Island since they were, after all, by a large body of water. Camp Good Days would be on an island. They decided who would play who and then went about the fun business of pretending to be that character.

"I think we should do something to get even with 'Batman,'" Erika said.

"Yeah. Let's get the 'Bat'," Yancy agreed.

The group liked the idea and began brainstorming.

After a quick badminton game and a swim in the lake, it was dinnertime. After dinner it was "Counselor Patrick's Mega-Monster Sundae" night again. Someone had crossed out the "Counselor Patrick" part and had magic-markered in "BATMAN's." As part of the joke, Patrick found some black cloth, cut a couple holes out for his eyes, and wore it over his face as he served up his famous sundaes.

"You look more like Zorro than Batman," one young camper said, looking up at the counselor.

Patrick responded by taking a spoon and carving the letter "Z" into the side of the camper's Sunday. "There. How do you like that?"

"Cool," the little one said with delight and went off to show his friends.

That night was the Improv Class's Show. The counselors, including Patrick, Marina, and Stency, sat amongst the children as the show got underway. Mrs. Maille was also seated in the gathering.

Just as the show was getting started, Marina spoke to Mrs. Maille and Stency. "I'm happy to see Luc has finally joined in the fun here. He's grown so much in only a few short days. He's opened up because of Erika for some reason."

"Erika seems to have grown, too," Stency added.

Mrs. Maille made a sweeping motion with her arm. With uncharacteristic enthusiasm she said, "This is wonderful place! Tres bien!"

A moment later someone onstage tossed a rubber snake into the air and it landed on the ground right beside her. Mrs. Maille jumped up and shrieked! "Mon Dieu! Je deteste les serpents! Va-t'en!"

The kids around her laughed.

Once Stency had removed the rubber snake and Marina had calmed Mrs. Maille down, it was show time.

Since it was her improv class, Stency stood up to introduce the play. "The children have named their play 'The Castaways Meet the Spacey Natives.'" She then announced, "Lights, music, and curtain, please."

Lights went up and a makeshift curtain parted.

"I'm GLilligan," Luc introduced himself. "I'm the Skipper's little buddy."

Mrs. Maille watched her son with a smile.

"I'm Merry Ann," Tully said. "I'm always happy."

Erika stepped forward and said, "I'm Oregano, the spicy movie star."

Yancy and Danny Flagpole stepped up next and said, "We're Mr. & Mrs. Wow!"

Marvin stood up, clicked his braces, and declared, "And I'm the professor. I'm the brainiest one on GLilligan's island."

Just then a couple of barefoot children wearing fake grass skirts appeared on the stage. They had gold-colored rings taped to the tips of their noses.

"Hey, these must be the natives of the island," Erika-Oregano suggested.

"Does anyone speak 'native'?" Mr. Wow-Danny asked.

"They're Tahitian," Mrs. Wow-Yancy declared.

"How can you tell they're Tahitian?" Mr. Wow asked. "Maybe they're from Borneo?"

"Easy, Darling. They have rings through their noses. I saw it in a magazine once. *Cosmo* or something chic like that," Mrs. Wow said with the wave of a hand.

"I know. Let me try," Luc-GLilligan said. He approached the natives and said, "Ooga boog-a."

Mrs. Maille caught herself laughing out loud and quickly covered her mouth.

"Ooga boog-a??" Erika-Oregano asked. "What does *that* mean?"

"It means, ooga-boog-a, who are you-a?" Luc answered.

The natives continued to remain speechless, staring off in the direction of the audience.

"I'll try," announced Professor Marvin. "Let me in here," he said as he wormed his way in between the other castaways.

"Yes. By all means," Erika-Oregano said to everyone. "Let the Professor try. He is a man of great knowledge! Plus he's so handsome. He'll know."

Professor Marvin stepped up to the natives and clicked his braces together. He then raised his hand as a symbol of peace and said, "Deklecto brasko."

The natives suddenly looked at each other and a smile broke across their otherwise stolid faces. "Deklecto brasko," they repeated and then they eagerly took the professor's hand and vigorously shook it.

Mr. Wow-Danny was astonished. "Amazing, my dear. He's knows how to talk the talk."

"What language is that professor?" Erika-Oregano asked

"It's outer space talk," Professor Marvin replied.

"You mean..." Oregano asked

"Yes, that's exactly what I mean."

"What? What does he mean?" Merry Ann-Tully asked.

"What on Earth are you all talking about?" Mr. Wow asked, growing impatient by the second.

"Not on Earth, Mr. Wow," Professor Marvin stated.

Mrs. Wow said, "You mean...?"

"Now, don't you start that again!" Mr. Wow snapped at his wife. "What does 'degalckto blasto' mean, anyway, and what did they say?"

Professor Marvin answered, "It doesn't mean they're from Tahiti, Mr. Wow. They are from outer space."

"They're aliens? Dressed like that? Rings through their noses and all? Give me a break!"

"It's true. These people are Polynoscoids. This is the way they dress."

"So, why are they here?" Merry Ann asked.

"To watch the movie *Plan 9 from Outer Space*," Marvin answered.

53

"Wait! Can they get us back to civilization in their spaceship?" Mr. Wow suddenly thought.

"No, it's impossible. They only have a coupe," Erika-Oregano answered.

Mr. Wow continued. "I'll give them a billion bucks if they let me climb in the wheel-well and get me off this dreadful rock! I can't stand these people anymore."

There was a moment of silence as the performers waited for delivery of the next line. It never came.

Mr. Wow shot a quick glance to offstage right, expecting the entrance of Bobby from cabin five. When Bobby from cabin five didn't materialize, Mr. Wow tried to look like nothing was wrong and he repeated his last line. "Like I said, I just can't stand these people anymore."

Again, Bobby from cabin five didn't appear on cue. For that matter he didn't appear at all. By now the entire cast was peering toward offstage right and didn't see anyone except Fred the stagehand. They even looked to offstage left, but, still, no one saw Bobby from cabin five.

The audience was well aware that the skit had taken an unexpected turn and everyone was looking at both sides of the stage expecting the absent cast member to suddenly appear.

"Well, where is he?" Counselor Patrick whispered to Marina.

Marina shrugged. "Beats me. What's going on here?"

Mrs. Maille was totally confused and she kept looking where everyone else was looking.

Onstage, Mr. Wow tried one more time. "I said - can you hear me BACK THERE?? - I can't stand these people anymore!"

The silence was broken when Fred the stagehand spoke in a whispered tone that everyone in the audience heard anyway. He said, "There's no one back here but me."

Just then the play was interrupted by a terrible scream. In the distance, someone was screaming and thrashing around in the lake.

"Hey! Someone is drowning in the lake!" Luc hollered.

Counselor Patrick jumped out of his seat and ran toward the lake. The other counselors and the children followed. When Patrick arrived he looked out into the darkened water. That's when he saw it. Something was floating nearly thirty-feet from shore. He thought it was a body and the counselor dove in.

As he swam toward the object, many of the other counselors and the children arrived, including Erika, Luc, Yancy, and Barnetta. Mrs. Maille was there as well. When Patrick arrived at the body he knew he had just been the victim of a prank. The clothes-laden Styrofoam dummy floated like a cork, but what gave the joke away was when he heard the raucous laughter from all of the kids ashore.

To the group of campers that had arrived on the beach, Yancy said, "Okay...one, two, three..."

In unison they shouted, "WELCOME TO GLILLIGAN'S ISLAND, BATMAN!"

"All right...very funny," Patrick said with good humor as he trudged ashore, splashing water up on the beach, and dragging his newfound dummy friend. "Revenge on the 'Batman'! I get it."

The children continued to laugh, including Bobby from cabin five who materialized on the beach.

"Good job, kids," he complimented them. "Good job. Got me good." Seeing Bobby from cabin five, Patrick said, "Oh, there you are, Bobby. I thought they had packed you away inside this Styrofoam thing here and sent you adrift."

"No, I'm still here," Bobby said, and laughed at the dripping wet counselor.

Patrick then noticed Barnetta holding her stuffed rabbit in her arms. She was laughing, too, but her laughter seemed weaker than usual. It made him pause with concern. Speaking like Bugs Bunny, Patrick said to her, "Hey, Doc...was that crazy wabbit involved in this, too?"

In the dim light on the beach, the little girl with red glasses shook her head no and smiled shyly at him.

"Okay, kids. The Improv show's over," Stency announced to everyone. "Time for the movie."

"Yes!" Marvin shouted with excitement. "*Plan 9* here we come!"

BAD NEWS

"This is the worst movie I've ever seen," Erika commented to Yancy as they watched fake-looking ghouls in a cardboard cemetery bumping into wobbly tombstones. Erika and Yancy were among nearly one hundred people gathered to watch the movie that night.

"You're right, Erika," Yancy agreed. "I don't think the counselors will ever listen to Marvin Tinkel again."

Halfway through the movie Erika noticed Counselor Sandi join the movie crowd. Sandi walked directly to Marina and whispered something in her ear. Marina then whispered something to Stency who was seated next to her. Stency looked at her suddenly; a wave of sadness passed over her face, but she quickly composed herself for the sake of those around her. Mrs. Maille was curious about what they were saying, but understood very little. A few moments later Marina and Sandi left the movie.

After the movie, Erika, Yancy, Tully, and Evy headed for their cabin, laughing about the prank Luc had pulled on his own mother. It had been Luc who had tossed the rubber snake at her from the stage.

"She must have thought it had fallen out of the tree," Evy laughed.

"She was so terrified! I couldn't believe it," Erika recalled. "Both Marina and Stency had to hug her to calm her down. They had to show her the snake wasn't real."

"A few more rubber snakes like that and Mrs. Maille will never want to come back to camp," Yancy added.

"'Le camp de bien d'jour, no tres bien,'" Tully said, attempting to mimic Mrs. Maille.

The girls laughed.

"Oui, oui, Mama. Ooo-la-la, chocolat," Evy said, throwing in the extent of her French.

"Hello, Mademoiselle Mama," Yancy said.

"Frere Jacques, Frere Jacques, dor mez vous, dor me vous?" Erika sang.

Before the girls had finished exploring their new language skills, they found themselves singing about "the girls in France don't wear underpants."

As the girls approached their cabin, they saw the lights were on.

"Looks like Barnetta's still up," Erika said.

"Why didn't she come to the movie?" Evy asked.

"Why would anybody want to see *that* movie," Yancy asked. "She probably saw it last year when Marvin bamboozled the counselors into showing it then."

When they entered the cabin the girls found Marina sitting on Barnetta's bunk. She was waiting for them. Barnetta was not there. Her bunk was neatly made and on the pillow sat her stuffed bunny rabbit.

"What's going on, Marina? Where's Barnetta?" Tully asked.

"That's why I'm here, girls. Barnetta became sick a little while ago and has been taken to the hospital in Syracuse."

"That bat really did bite her," Evy suggested. There was fear in her tone.

"No, Evy," Marina said compassionately. "The bat didn't bite her. Her illness is the reason she is sick."

The girls looked at one another, uncertain as to what to say; though, they knew words were not required. They all lived under the same shadow.

"Is she going to be okay?" Yancy asked.

"I truly don't know, Yancy. She was a very sick girl, as you know. All we can do is hope for the best and pray for her."

The girls nodded.

Erika noticed Barnetta's stuffed bunny rabbit still sitting on the pillow. She optimistically said, "She left her bunny rabbit, so she must be planning on coming back, Marina."

Marina smiled and looked at the rabbit. "Must be so," she said, returning the optimistic gesture; but then she noticed a small piece of paper tied around the stuffed bunny's neck. She handled the paper and when she saw one side was blank, she flipped it over. There she saw writing. Marina read the words that had been hand-written. She was immediately saddened and covered her mouth. She took a deep breath in an attempt to hold back her tears.

The girls couldn't help but notice.

"What's it say, Marina?" Erika asked.

After a moment, Marina answered, "It says...'For Counselor Patrick.'"

"What's it mean?" Tully asked.

"It means she left her bunny rabbit to him," Yancy said.

"It means she didn't think she'd be coming back," Erika added with sadness.

The next morning came early as Erika, Yancy, Tully, and Evy, were rousted out of their bunks at 6:30 by Stency. They had signed up to do a "Polar Bear" swim before breakfast.

"Rise and shine, girls!" the counselor called out as she entered the cabin and woke everyone. "Time for a brisk swim in the lake!" Satisfied that everyone's eyes were open, Stency then moved on to the next cabin that had signed up.

As the four girls rose and donned their swimsuits, they all noticed the empty bunk in the cabin and were reminded of Marina's bad news last night about Barnetta.

"I wonder how she's doing?" Tully asked no one in particular.

"Maybe Marina or Patrick can find out for us," Erika suggested.

On the walk to the lake, the girls asked Stency if she had heard anything about Barnetta, but Stency replied she had not.

Despite the fact that it was summertime, going for a swim in the lake the first thing in the morning was still a bone-chilling experience. A couple dozen campers jumped into the sixty-eight degree lake and most were momentarily shocked by the lake's relatively cold temperature. Goose bumps ruled the morning.

Shivering all the way back to the cabin after the brief swim, Erika said, "Well, now that I've done that, there's no need to do it again."

Her cabin mates quickly agreed with her.

Patrick received the call from Syracuse shortly after breakfast. After he had hung up, he debated whether or not to tell anyone the news. He knew the campers would be asking how Barnetta was doing and he couldn't very well lie about it.

He wiped the tears from his eyes and left his office. He headed out to inform all of the counselors, and then to find the girls of cabin six.

It was morning break time and Erika, Yancy, Tully, and Evy were in their cabin writing postcards to home when Marina and Patrick knocked on their door.

"Come in," Yancy said.

Marina and Patrick entered.

When Tully saw Patrick she said, "There aren't any bats in here today, Patrick."

Patrick laughed. "That's good to hear. I didn't feel like doing any big-time wrestling with another bat today." He looked around the room and then, turning more serious, he said, "Girls, the reason we're here is I have some bad news to tell you."

"Barnetta?" Yancy asked.

Patrick nodded. "Yes. She didn't make it. She died a short time ago; while we were having breakfast."

"No," Erika said quietly.

Tully, Evy, and Yancy remained silent, lost in their own thoughts; tears welling up in their eyes.

Patrick saw their looks of sadness. He continued. "I feel the same as you about it, girls. I'm sorry I had to tell you. I just felt that you should know. You were her roommates. I'm very sad, just as you are, that she is gone. We will all miss her. I also want you to know that these things happen, and we have to accept them. I want all of you to make it a point to have a great time for the rest of the week you are here. Have fun for Barnetta's sake and, please, don't let her passing get you down. She'd want you all to have a good time. I know she would. Okay, girls?"

Each of the girls mumbled, "Okay."

"Okay." Patrick and Marina then left the cabin.

The word spread faster than email and by lunchtime everyone in camp knew. In no time at all the mood throughout the camp was down. Many of the campers' minds were not on their activities. The invisible shadow which hovered over all suddenly was visible. All of the counselors saw it in the eyes of the campers. The kids weren't as responsive or as interested as in the previous days. Even the counselors were affected and their spirits were low. By afternoon break time many counselors immediately went to Patrick and told him of their feelings.

"We have to do something," Sandi said.

"Everyone seems so depressed and sad," Stency observed.

"We must do something to improve the situation before these campers go home," Marina said to Patrick.

Patrick agreed. "Kids are here just to enjoy life and forget about cancer for a while. I'm sorry the kids found out, but everyone wanted to know how Barnetta was doing. I just couldn't lie about it."

"No, that wouldn't have been the right thing to do," Marina said, trying to make Patrick feel better. She knew Barnetta's passing was especially hard on him. "But what can we do now?"

Patrick thought for a moment. He then said to them, "I know what to do."

Patrick was a caring counselor who always sought to make sure the campers had a good time. He quickly recognized the need to hold a special service in Barnetta's memory in order to help the campers deal with the bad news. A uniting. Otherwise, he feared, many of the campers' experience could be tarnished or ruined for the summer.

Just before dinner, Patrick's friend Reverend Flory arrived from Rochester and a brief memorial service was held at the camp's outdoor chapel. Everyone in the camp attended. The outdoor chapel was set beside a small creek in a remote and quiet area in the woods. At the head of the chapel stood - side by side - both a wooden Star of David and a Christian cross. As Reverend Flory spoke about "remembering another brave soul who lost her battle," Erika noticed at the foot of each religious symbol there was a small mound made up of flat rocks. Each flat rock had a name hand-written on it. The Reverend, at one point during the service, referred to them as the memorial rocks.

Erika then noticed Luc and his mother standing nearby. Mrs. Maille was crying as she held tightly to Luc's hand. She dabbed a wrinkled Kleenix to her eyes. Luc rubbed his mother's back in an effort to comfort her as they listened to Reverend Flory.

"I spoke with Barnetta's parents today," Reverend Flory said. "As you all may have known, Barnetta was very sick. And yet she lived longer than anyone had expected or could have hoped for. Her parents believe it was the camp that kept her going. They said she was so excited and looked so forward to coming to camp every summer. Her parents believe that the camp, with all of you providing warmth and camaraderie and just plain, old-fashioned fun, had given her reason to live, and reason to hope. Her parents are grateful to each and every one of you for making this place so special for her and making her last few days so much fun."

After the service ended, Erika and her cabin mates took time to each write Barnetta's name on a rock and they placed them on top of the hundreds of other memorial rocks that had been placed on the ground over the years at the foot of the Christian cross and the Star of David.

Despite the dark shadow of sadness that covered the camp that day, the counselors worked extra hard playing with the children. They engaged them in busy evening activities to help take their minds off the sad news and to make sure the rest of their time at camp was fun-filled and magical. Counselor Patrick worked especially hard to fulfill every counselor's goal of making sure the kids were there just to enjoy life. He had been particularly saddened by Barnetta's passing because she had left her bunny rabbit to him. He never fully realized how much the quiet little girl had appreciated him.

Patrick and his counselors' efforts paid off. By the end of the evening the camp was full of laughter and mischief again. The memorial service with Reverend Flory had done wonders to buoy everyone's spirits. The evening improv skits went on as planned in the recreation center. Erika and her roommates, along with Luc, laughed as they watched their camp mates pretend they were the Dragnet agents in pursuit of a stolen fax machine.

The improvs were immediately followed by the weekly camp dance, complete with a disk jockey, a rotating silver-mirrored ball light in the middle of the ceiling, and a small bank of flashing, colored strobe lights. Erika and Luc danced with each other to the throbbing sound of the loud music. Erika showed Luc some of the latest American dances, though Luc didn't think they looked much different than dances he had seen in France. Even Mrs. Maille was kicking up her heels on the dance floor. She was dancing with Patrick; her earlier sadness replaced by laughter.

Later Erika and Luc went outside and joined another group of campers and counselors who were making s'mores around the huge campfire, telling stories, and singing songs like the "Titanic" song. The evening had turned into a party and everyone in the camp was having a warm-spirited and wonderful time.

When Marina returned to her cabin after the dance had ended and the last ember in the campfire had gone out, she discovered someone had filled her sleeping bag with corn flakes. She laughed and said to herself aloud, "All right, who's the wise guy?"

She was pleased. She knew the camp was back on track again.

TIME TO LEAVE

It was their last chess game beside the lake before the week was over.

"It's your move, Erika," Luc said.

"I'm scared, Luc," she said.

"About what?"

"I said I wasn't but I am. I worry about my family and my dog. I love my mom and dad and I worry they'll always feel sad over me. I don't want them to be unhappy. I worry that Michele might forget to feed Mooflee. I worry that Mooflee might get lonely."

"I used to think things like that, too. But I don't now. There's nothing I can do about them."

"You act as though you don't care about your family."

"I *do* care," Luc said with reassurance. "I'm like you. I love my parents. But by not being scared I *feel* better. I can do *more* with myself while I can." Luc added, "The fear doesn't waste my time anymore."

Erika didn't say anything. She could sense the truth in what Luc said.

"See those kids?" Luc asked, pointing to four children in wheelchairs gathered nearby beside the lake. They were talking, joking, and watching the passing boats. "There's Randy, Melinda, Ursala, and Sam. All of them don't have much time left. You're lucky, Erika. You're better off than most. So, take chances you've never taken before. This might be your last time to do things."

When Erika didn't say anything, he added, "It's okay to be scared. There isn't a person here who isn't. Just don't let the fear waste your time."

Erika smiled and made her next move. "I'll miss you, Luc. I'm going to try to come back as soon as I can."

"I hope you do."

It was the last night of camp and the traditional memorial lighting of candles was held beside the lake after sunset. All of the campers were invited to participate. The memorial was to those who weren't coming back. The memorial was also a way to slow things down at the camp on the last night. After a very busy week at camp, it was time for the kids to wind down, to reflect on the past week, and to think about going back home and to the uncertainties and challenges of the weeks ahead. It also served as a way for the campers to say good-bye to each other after a fun-filled week of activities, adventures, and, most importantly, camaraderie.

Erika and her fellow campers were each given an unlit candle. Erika listened as a brief presentation was made by the camp's founder, a nice, old gentleman who, himself, had lost a daughter to cancer. In the light of the candle the founder held in his hand, he spoke of the good things in people's lives and how important it was to remember your friends. He wished everyone well, and then he turned to the camper standing next to him and lit his candle. That camper, in turn, lit the next camper's candle, and so on, the flame was passed. Yancy lit Erika's, and Erika lit Luc's. After all of the candles were lit and, after a brief period of quiet, the candles were set, one by one, on the beach.

Erika followed Luc and placed hers beside the lengthening row of candles forming along the edge of the water. In what seemed like no time at all, a line of one-hundred and fifty candles were burning brightly along the Finger Lake's shoreline, illuminating everybody.

Erika, Luc, and their fellow campers joined hands, forming a human chain behind the candle-lit breakwater. It was a solemn time. While some children spoke quietly of absent friends, others stood silently content with their own thoughts and feelings. Some kids gazed at the star-studded sky above and made secret wishes. In the background were the ever-present sounds of water lapping up on the shore, bullfrogs, and crickets.

As the candles eventually burned out, the human chain began to quietly break apart. Erika, Yancy, Tully, and Evy all hugged each other in memory of their lost cabin mate Barnetta. They all shed tears.

The campers then drifted off in many directions. Some sat on the beach to reflect and talk. Others headed to the chow hall where junk food heaven was underway. The chow hall was open late on that last night and unlimited ice cream, soda, and pizza were just a few of the mouth-watering entrees being offered. Other campers headed for their cabins and to bed.

The next morning it was time to leave. The yellow bus was standing by, waiting to take the children back to where their journeys had begun. Everyone in the camp was gathered around it, cheering and clapping, just as they had when they arrived. Clowns, counselors, kids. Luc and his mother were there, too.

"Au revoir, Erika," Mrs. Maille said with a smile.

"Good-bye, Mrs. Maille," Erika said. To Luc, "Good-bye, Luc. You have my phone number and address. Please write or call me."

"I will," he said with assurance, and then he hugged his friend. "Good-bye."

Erika and Yancy bid farewell to their roommates and gave each of them a hug.

After the hugs were done, Evy said, "I thought you might like this, Erika." She handed her a drawing from her sketchbook.

Erika took the drawing and looked at it. It was a detailed pencil drawing of her and Luc playing at the chess table with the lake in the background.

"Oh, this is so good, Evy," Erika said. She was touched by her roommate's thoughtfulness. "Thank you so much. I'll always keep it."

"You're quite welcome," Evy said.

Climbing aboard the bus, Erika waved to all of her new friends and the counselors. Everyone, including Tully and Evy, waved back. Their own bus would be taking them home later that same morning. The yellow bus then headed down the road and Erika watched as the camp disappeared behind it.

An hour later the bus arrived back in Canandaigua. Erika gathered her things and headed for the door.

"Bye, Yancy," Erika said to her new friend. She and Yancy had become as close as sisters in such a very short time.

"Let's stay in touch," Yancy said. "I'm just down in Naples."

"Okay."

When Erika stepped off the bus her mom and dad were there to pick her up. They were surprised, yet pleased to see Erika was excited and bursting with energy.

"Hi Mom! Hi Dad! That was a fun place," she announced as she gave them both hugs. "Can I go back again soon?"

Her parents were speechless as they looked at each other. There were happy the week had been such a big success. Mr. Reisling could only answer, "Sure, Erika. I don't see why not."

The yellow bus began pulling away. Erika waved at Yancy who waved back.

INVENTIONS AND COOKIES

The Girl Scout cookie order forms were spread out on the kitchen table. Like a small platoon going out on an important mission, Erika & Co. prepared to move out. They folded the order forms and placed them in their backpacks. They were excited and were going to sell cookies to the whole world by going door to door. Well, maybe not the whole world they decided, scaling back a bit, but at least to the neighborhood at hand.

Erika and her two friends told each other camp stories as they went from house to house. Melanie and Jo had both been to camps, too, that month. All three girls talked about the new friends they had made and the fun times they had experienced. They talked about the sing-alongs around the campfires and the making of the s'mores. They agreed the s'mores were among the best parts.

She told her friends about some of the fun things they had done. Volleyball, Ping-Pong, movie night, mega-sundaes, tennis with Tully, swimming, go-carts, and pranks. Melanie and Jo listened with great interest and delight to the tales of bats, rubber snakes, and Styrofoam bodies. She also told them about Barnetta.

"One of my roommates died."

"What happened?" Jo asked.

"Yeah, how'd she die?" Melanie asked.

"She had leukemia," Erika answered, matter-of-factly.

"Like yours?" Melanie asked, concerned.

"Yeah...sort of like mine," Erika said, trying to avoid sounding solemn as she considered the recent news of her own relapse. "Except hers was more advanced and the treatments weren't working. They said she had some 'complications,' too; whatever that means."

"What about *your* treatments, Erika?" Jo demanded to know.

"Yeah, are they working?" Melanie was quick to follow-up.

Not wanting to alarm her friends, she replied, "Yes, they're working." Shrugging her shoulders, she added, "I'm not worried." She then announced, "Someday we should *all* go to the *same* camp...together."

"Yeah, we should," Jo agreed with enthusiasm.

"Why didn't we think of that before?" Melanie asked.

Suddenly, there was an awkward moment of silence amongst the three friends. The girls - including Erika - suddenly felt a somber wave pass through them as they each wondered how many of those "somedays" were really left.

For nearly an hour the girls trekked from house to house selling cookies. They did quite well, too. An hour-and-a-half's worth of peddling and pitching had yielded an astonishing fifty-three orders among them. As they bicycled to their next target, they suddenly came upon Brian "Doc" Beyer and his mother getting out of their car.

"Hey, there's Doc," Erika said. "Come on."

Doc and his mom were carrying groceries into the house. It was easy spotting Doc from a distance because he was one large boy. He loved to eat and even though he was only twelve, he was as big as a sixteen-year-old. Most of his friends thought the reason he ate so much was simply to fuel his high-energy brain.

They had heard Doc's story at what was now being called "Peggy's Food Fight Birthday Party" and so they were anxious to hear if it was true. They knew something was up because they hadn't seen him in days.

"Hi, Doc!" Erika said, riding to and coming to a stop beside him.

"Hey! Hi, Erika," he replied. He was very happy to see his friends. "Hi Melanie. Hi Jo."

"Hi, Doc," Melanie said, pulling up beside Erika.

"Hey, Doc," Jo returned his greeting.

"How are you doing, Erika?" Doc asked, very interested in his friend's well being. "Still hanging in there?"

"I'm still on my bike, aren't I?" Erika replied with a smile.

"You'll beat it," he said reassuringly. "I know you will."

Changing the subject, Erika asked, "Where have you been? Peggy Winkleman said you were 'taken away.'"

"I was! I just got back from the FBI's."

Jo asked, "The FBI? What did you do?"

"Oh, nothin' much," he said. "I broke into some silly government defense computer using my iMac."

"I told ya," Melanie said to the others. "What did they do to you?"

"They wanted to know how I did it, and then they threatened to give me a lobotomy and send me to a place for bad kids if I did it again. So I promised I wouldn't do it again." Then adding with emphasis, he winked and said, "Not!" He then laughed like Ernie on *Sesame Street*.

Jo asked, "What's a 'lobotomy'?"

"Oh, not much, really. That's where they take an eggbeater, slip it into the corner of your head, and flick the switch. When they turn it off, you don't know up from down or what channel *Nickelodeon* is on."

Jo was horrified. "Uh!"

"What did your dad say?" Erika wanted to know.

"Nothing yet. He's not home. He's on assignment in the Soviet Union with the CIA spying on the Russian mafia. Or, so he says. Hey, I've got something I want to show you all. Come with me."

The girls went to Doc's laboratory which was located down in the basement of the Beyer home. It was known by the kids in the neighborhood as the "Doc Room," although it seemed more like a dark dungeon. The Doc Room had bubbling water flowing through glass tubes like something lifted off an old-fashioned *Frankenstein* movie set. On his workbench the girls saw an odd-looking bow and arrow set. The arrows were wired and there were some tiny circuit boards strapped to them. There was also a television set, a VCR, and a whole bunch other electronic stuff and parts scattered on the bench. Most everything looked like nothing more than junk.

Doc recklessly pushed aside a handful of the nondescript parts from the middle of the bench, found one part of particular interest, and picked it up. It was a small electronic device of some sort. He said, "I was working on this just before they took me away." He reached over and turned on the television and the VCR.

"What is it?" Erika asked.

"It's a CCD. It's like a miniaturized TV camera. It's what makes a camcorder work." Doc took the tiny device, clipped it to the tip of one of the arrows, and connected some wires to it. He clicked another switch and suddenly a picture of the basement appeared on the television. He then pointed the arrow at them and the girls suddenly saw themselves on television.

"Wow! That's neat," Melanie said.

"Gee, that is a tiny camera," Erika observed. "That's cool."

"Yeah. It is kinda cool, ha-ha," he laughed, delighted with his own creation.

Doc then pressed the record button on the VCR and picked up the bow.

"Now watch this," he said gleefully.

He placed the arrow on the bow's guide, drew the arrow back, and took aim at a plastic model of the *SS Enterprise* that was hanging on a string in the corner.

The girls watched as he drew the bowstring tight and then saw the *Enterprise* appear on the television.

"Space! The Final Frontier!" Doc announced, and then released the arrow.

The arrow shot through the air and hit the model dead-on. SHHOOM-CRASH!

The girls were stunned as it smashed the model into a gazillion pieces, which were then scattered all over the cellar floor.

Doc laughed and tossed the bow back on the bench.

"Blam! Utter obliteration! And now watch this." He reached over to the VCR and pressed a couple of buttons. "You can even watch it over again on the playback, and in slow motion, too!"

They all watched the screen. It appeared they were flying through the basement with great speed and then collided with the space ship. The screen then went blank upon impact.

Erika said, "That's kind of cool."

"Thanks!" Doc said, proudly.

"But what good is it?" she asked.

"I don't know. I was just playing around one day when I had nothing to do. Haven't thought of a use for it yet. So, what are you guys doing?"

Erika said, "Selling cookies. Wanna buy some?"

"Mmmm, yeah," Doc said. "Talk to my mom."

"Okay," Erika said as they headed up the stairs. "Come on over sometime."

"Mom won't let me for a while. She hasn't been happy with me lately. I'm grounded until dad gets home and the FBI stops calling. But I'll try."

THE SALES PITCH

As the girls bicycled back to Erika's house, Erika stopped at the foot of the McGillacuddy's driveway.

"Too bad Doc's mom grounded him," Erika said.

"Yeah. He's going to miss out on some of the summer," Melanie said.

"Why are you stopping here?' Jo asked.

Erika tossed a glance in the direction of the McGillacuddy mansion.

"No," Jo said in disbelief. "You're not going up *there*, are you?"

"Sure," Erika said and smiled. "Why not? It's for a good cause, isn't it?"

"I don't know," Melanie said, doubtful.

"Hey, all she can say is no," Erika pointed out.

Melanie smiled, the mischief in her appearing. She turned her bike around and headed for the McGillacuddy's driveway. "Come on, Jo. It'll be memorable. Let's do it, Erika."

"All right," Jo said and peddled into the driveway.

"Jo and I will be right behind you," Melanie said.

The three girls parked their bicycles at the foot of the mansion's large wooden steps and looked up in awe at the size of this ominous, old Victorian wonder. It was the closest any of them had ever come to this place in their lives and they all felt a little scared that they had actually come this far into forbidden territory. They took a deep breath and Erika led the way up the steps to the porch and then to the massive front door. She raised the heavy, brass doorknocker and rapped the plate beneath it. The thick, wooden door resonated. Many long, long moments passed...and then they heard the latch being moved. The door slowly opened. The girls didn't know what to expect. Jo expected to see some monstrous, oozy creature from outer space. Melanie envisioned a well-dressed, eight-feet tall butler named Lurch. Erika imagined she'd see the Wicked Witch of the West with a long, pointy nose with a green wart on its tip. Instead, the girls found themselves face to face with Mrs. McGillacuddy herself.

She wasn't gaunt and eight-feet tall, nor was she monstrous and alien. What she was was an overweight woman of average size, longish hair, and wearing heavy, pasty make-up on her face which gave her a painted, mannequin look. This veneer did not improve the dour cast on her face, nor did it mask the harsh, deep lines and wrinkles. These could only have come from years of scowling and grimacing, and just plain-old being mean and angry.

Mrs. McGillacuddy did not smile when she saw the children. She eyed them with fury which did give her the witch-like appearance Erika had expected.

"What do you children want here?" she blustered.

Erika remained calm and spoke first.

"Good evening, Mrs. McGillacuddy. We're selling Girl Scout cookies. Would you like to buy some?"

Mrs. McGillacuddy bellowed, "You must be kidding! You girls have a lot of nerve riding up my driveway on your bicycles and asking *me* for money."

"Yes, Ma'am," Erika agreed wholeheartedly.

"It is for a good cause, Mrs. McGillacuddy" Melanie added.

"And the cookies taste really good, too," Jo chimed in.

Mrs. McGillacuddy was not at all impressed or amused. "Take your wasted little lives and get off of my property. Now!"

Erika studied this horrible woman for a moment and was surprised to find herself not offended by the comment. In fact, quite the contrary. She said, "I feel very sorry for you, Mrs. McGillacuddy. You're just a poor, old selfish woman who doesn't appreciate anything or anyone. I'm sorry, but *you're* the one whose life's been a waste."

Jo's and Melanie's jaws had dropped. They were speechless. Their faces had a "Like wow!" expression glued all over them.

Erika quietly turned to leave. "Come on, girls. Let's go."

Mrs. McGillacuddy herself was momentarily stunned and was speechless as well. She finally blurted out to the departing children, "Why...I-I've never in my whole life encountered such a disrespectful little girl as you Erika Reisling! I'm going to tell your father!" She then promptly slammed the heavy door to their backs. It made a deep, resounding crash.

"Whew," Jo said, relieved. "I told you we shouldn't have come."

Erika said, "Don't feel bad, Jo. She did the same thing to my mom a long time ago."

"I knew Mil-Dread wouldn't buy any cookies," Melanie added smugly. "But it was fun. Did you 'Wow' her! Did you see her face when Erika told her that *her* life was a waste? She didn't know what to say! The 'Dread was speechless!"

"Gosh, does she remind you of that wicked old witch in 'The Wizard of Oz' or what?" Erika observed.

Jo added, "She reminds me of that old lady who rode the bicycle in the 'Wizard of Oz.'"

Melanie said, "They're the same person, silly."

Melanie and Erika giggled and all the girls went home.

In the McGillacuddy mansion Mrs. McGillacuddy returned to the huge library where she had left her husband.

"Who was that, Mildred?" Cecil McGillacuddy asked his wife when she entered the room. He was sitting in his tall chair sipping a drink and reading a book.

"Just that pesty little riffraff child next door who owns that awful animal."

"What did she want?" he asked.

"She wanted to sell me cookies or some such tripe."

Cecil returned to his drink and his book.

Mrs. M continued. "I hate that disgusting, mangy-looking animal. It fouls our lovely gardens and should be taken away. It belongs in a cage at the Humane Society."

"She's just a harmless, friendly sheepdog, Mildred," her husband said.

"Harmless?" she said raising her voice. Mrs. McGillacuddy fawned over a broken flower she had brought in earlier from the garden. "That animal broke the stem of my prize-winning tea rose, imported all of the way from England. My beautiful British Bell," she moaned. "Poor little thing."

"Anything could have broken it, Dear. Perhaps one of the guests from the other day," he said, unaware he was rubbing the side of his leg where he had been pricked by the rose bush. "Some were a bit tipsy."

"Ha! Our guests would never be so clumsy, Cecil."

"Whatever you say, Dear."

He took a big sip of his drink and returned to his book.

Mrs. McGillacuddy snipped and trimmed the tea rose. As she placed it in a vase with tepid water after angling the stem just so, she snapped, "Cecil, you're book is upside down again."

"Oh?" he asked. Realizing she was right, he turned the book right side up. "Thank you, Dear."

CECIL & MOOFLEE

The next day Mr. McGillacuddy appeared in the rear grounds near the hedgerow. In his hand was a small paper bag. He walked to the hedgerow and peeked through. He looked around the Reisling's backyard until he found what he was searching for. Quietly resting on the grass was Mooflee.

"Here...doggie," he said in a low voice to Erika's dog. "Heeerrre, doggie, doggie, doggie."

Mooflee heard him and her ears perked. She rose from her rest spot and slowly approached the hedgerow to investigate. Mr. McGillacuddy pulled a steak from a bag. It was getting a little too risky for him to continue burying the steaks - with Mildred and the gardeners never being far away - so he graduated to just plain feeding the dog.

"I've got a present for you, doggie."

Smelling the steak, Mooflee eagerly climbed through the hole in the hedge. Once through, Mr. McGillacuddy gave her the steak.

"Gooood doggie," Mr. McGillacuddy said happily as he petted the dog. "That's a girl. Goood doggie. Eat your present."

Mooflee was grateful for the treat.

Just then Mrs. McGillacuddy's shrill voice pierced the air. "Cecil!" she called out from the house.

Mooflee froze in mid-bite with the steak hanging from her mouth.

Mr. McGillacuddy froze, too.

"Oops," he said, not wanting to get caught.

"Cecil! Where are you?" the voice beckoned.

"Coming, Dear," he finally called back. To Mooflee, he said with urgency, "Go on, now. Shoo! Go! Get out of here!"

Mooflee took the beef and jumped back through the hole as Mr. McGillacuddy hurried to attend his wife.

THE REISLING HOUSE

"Erika, the McGillacuddy's called again," Mr. Reisling said. "Mrs. McGillacuddy said your were rude to her."

Erika said, "Dad, all I did was try to sell her Girl Scout cookies. Melanie and Jo were with me."

"They also said Mooflee was in their yard again. I'm afraid we'll have to make a doggy run and hook her up to it. She said next time she will call the dogcatcher. I wish I knew why that dog keeps going over there."

Erika walked over to Mooflee, knelt down, and hugged her. "Why are you going over there, you moose?? Do you want to be tied up?" When the dog didn't answer, Erika headed for the stairs. Mooflee followed.

"I'm getting very tired of those people calling us all of the time with their complaints," Mrs. Reisling said. "The old snobs. First, they complain about our yard, then they complain about our car and how it looks old. And now they complain about our little girl and dog. I sometime think they're just trying to drive us out of here. I've had just about enough of their nonsense."

Mr. Reisling looked sympathetically at his wife. "Come on," he spoke gently. "You're upset, Honey. You know nothing they say makes any difference."

"I know," she said. "It just makes me mad, that's all. That woman thinks her neighbors are too blue collar for her blue blood."

"Yes, and so what if she does? Who cares?"

"You're right," Mrs. Reisling said. "She doesn't matter. I just don't like anyone saying bad things about Erika."

"I don't either."

When Erika and Mooflee reached the top of the stairs, Erika heard a "psss-psss" sound. She looked down the darkened hallway. It was coming from Michele's room.

Erika quietly stepped into her sister's room and found Michele awake in bed. "Michele, what's up?"

"I heard loud voices," her little sister said. "Are mom and dad fighting?"

"No, they're not. Everything's okay," Erika reassured her.

"Erika?"

"What?"

"Did you give Mooflee a steak from the refrigerator yesterday?"

"Of course not," Erika laughed. "What would make you think that?"

"After you left to sell cookies, I saw Mooflee chewing on a steak in the front yard by the hedge."

"Maybe dad gave it to her."

"Maybe," Michele said. "I didn't want to ask him because I didn't want to get you in trouble."

"Thanks for thinking of me, Sis," Erika said appreciatively.

"Hey, we have to look out for each other."

"That's for sure," Erika agreed. "Oh, I'm going away to camp again next week."

"Again? Boy, lucky you."

"So, you keep an eye on Mooflee. Make sure she doesn't get into any trouble. Okay?"

"Okay," Michele answered.

LUC THE WISE

Erika jumped off the yellow Camp Good Days bus. Counselors Marina and Patrick greeted her.

"Welcome back, Erika!" Marina said.

"Hi Marina! I told you I'd come back. Which cabin am I in?"

"I can tell you don't want to waste any time," the counselor said with delight. Marina took a quick glance at her clipboard. "I've assigned you to your old cabin again. Cabin six. With Yancy."

"Yancy's back? Wow! Great! What about Luc? Is he here?"

"Yes...he's here," the counselor answered with some hesitation. "I know he's looking forward to seeing you, Erika."

"Well, I want to see him," Erika said happily. She took her backpack and headed for the cabin. "Thank you, Marina."

Marina had wanted to say something to her about Luc, but Erika was already running back to her old cabin. She knew Erika would find out soon enough.

Erika placed her stuff on her old bed in cabin six and then headed off for the lake. She found Luc in his usual place sitting at the chess table by the lake.

"Luc!" she called out, delighted to see him, and she ran to the lake.

Mrs. Maille was gathering a snack for Luc in the main lodge when she heard her son's name called out. She looked outside and saw Erika running toward him.

As Erika approached Luc she was stunned when she saw him. Luc wasn't sitting in the chair beside the chess table. He was seated in a wheelchair. Erika looked at his face. The friendly face beneath the purple scarf he wore on his head was paler and not quite as alert. His condition had grown worse since she had last seen him over a month ago.

"Erika," he said happily when he saw her. His voice was weak. "Hi!"

They hugged each other and she sat down across from him.

Mrs. Maille's eyes swelled with tears as she watched from the lodge's doorway.

"How are you?" Erika asked her friend.

"I'm okay. I just can't get around as much," Luc said motioning to the chair.

"What happened?"

Luc shrugged. "Nothing. It's just those little demons running around in my head eating up my brain again. The doctor at Hopkins couldn't get them all. I guess they're having a feast. But, 'oh well.'"

"Luc, I'm sorry."

"Ah, don't worry about it," he said dismissing the problem lamely with his hand. "I was hoping I'd see you here again. I'm glad you came back. My chess was getting rusty. Let's play."

The two children set up their chess pieces and began playing against the peaceful backdrop of the lovely, warm summer afternoon beside the lake.

Mrs. Maille arrived with snacks for the two of them. She greeted Erika and then sat down to watch the children play their game.

The week went quickly. Erika noticed right away that Luc's spirits had weakened since her last camp visit. She found herself helping him and she made it her goal to pump his spirits up.

There were many stories and s'mores around the nightly campfires. It was mid-August and the Earth's orbit was intersecting the center of a stream of particles in space which produced the annual Perseids meteor shower. One night it was spectacularly clear and the children saw dozens of meteors, one right after the other, shooting across the night sky. It was a glorious and magical event which kept everyone - campers and counselors alike - up for hours after lights out. More wishes were made on that night than on any other. Especially Erika. She made a wish with every single shooting star she saw.

Erika and Luc went fishing off the dock and caught nothing. The fish, as usual, had a feast and swam off with their fat, juicy worms. The dinner bell was rung, dinner was served, and afterwards counselor Patrick made his Mega-Monster Sundaes. Erika would fetch one for Luc and surprise him with it.

Luc's mom worried constantly about her son and was hovering about him most of the time. Erika would push him around in his wheelchair and Mrs. Maille would always be saying, "Be careful! Sois prudent!"

Erika would just as often reassure her by replying, "Don't worry, Mrs. Maille."

Movie nights weren't the same without freckle-faced Marvin Tinkel begging for a science fiction movie and both Erika and Luc realized they missed his brace-clicking, "Gort" impersonation. They had heard from the counselors that Marvin was doing okay and that he was making progress. That made them feel better. Despite Marvin's absence, the film selections for the camp's "Movies Under the Stars" nights were good. One night Agnieszka Holland's *The Secret Garden* was shown on the big canvas screen and, on another night, they showed *Inspector Gadget* to the campers.

Later that night, long after the movies had ended, Erika and her roommates were in their bunks fast asleep. Suddenly, they were awakened by the sound of the camp's bell. It began ringing for no reason at all. They all sat up in their bunks and looked at each other.

"What's going on?" Yancy asked.

Erika and her roommates got up and turned on their flashlights. They slowly stepped outside of their cabin and looked around. They saw the other kids in all of the other cabins coming outside. The bell continued to ring. Standing in their nightgowns and pajamas, they all noticed the playing field was beginning to glow. They all headed for the field. That's when they noticed something miraculous was happening to each other. As the bell rang, the kids' "shackles" suddenly began to fall away. Canes and crutches dropped to the ground. Braces came apart and fell to the ground in pieces. Slings around limp arms were tossed into the air, along with eye patches and bandages. Kids slowly rose from their wheelchairs and pushed them away. Kids rose from their sick beds and came outdoors. Illnesses disappeared. Pain and weakness were replaced by joy and strength. All of the campers were suddenly free from the shackles that had brought them to this wonderful camp in the first place. One by one they rejoiced the miracle that had taken place and they walked, hopped, skipped, and jumped toward the middle of the camp's playfield. The glow in the field intensified and the children danced the night away in an aura of brilliant golden white light. Out of nowhere the sky was suddenly filled with small bits of sparkling gold confetti. It was as though it were snowing gold everywhere. Some landed on Erika's shoulder. When she brushed it off, she realized that not only was there gold confetti on her shoulder, but also her own light brown *hair*. It had grown back to its fullness!

"Is it a miracle or is it heaven?" Erika wondered. Who knew? Who cared? It didn't matter!

She ran to Luc's cabin and found him outside sitting in his wheelchair. Luc was watching, bedazzled by the euphoria occurring around him, when Erika suddenly appeared in front of him.

He stared at her, amazement in his eyes, for what seemed like a long time and then said, "Erika...you have hair!"

"I know!" she laughed as she played with her hair. "Isn't it wonderful?"

Luc removed the scarf on his head. Erika was astounded to see that the scars on his head were healed and his hair had returned!

"You have hair, too!" she said.

She held out her hand to him. He took it and she helped him up. He suddenly realized that he was *all right* and didn't need her help! He was fine!

"Come on, Luc!" Erika said excitedly. "Come on!"

The two laughed and then hurried toward the center of the playing field with all of the other children who were now dancing in one large circle. The brilliant, golden white light was warm and beautiful and they were all bathed in it. And the moments went on, and on, and on. For what seemed like most of the night. A night with lots of laughter and magic. Kids were doing cartwheels. Others were doing somersaults. The gold confetti continued to snow down on them all.

And then...

...the gold confetti stopped...

...and then, like the stroke of midnight in "Cinderella," the camp's bell began ringing again.

Erika heard it first and she glanced in the bell's direction. A child was tugging at the bell rope. The child was sad. The brilliant golden light began to change and all of the children looked up. It began to soften and fade away. The playing field was becoming darker.

Erika shook her head and uttered, "Please, no..."

And then all of the children knew what was happening. They suddenly stopped their dancing. One by one, they slowly turned around and, with heads hung low, headed back to their cabins. The warm golden light overhead faded, becoming cold blue, and then dark.

"No," Erika repeated as Luc looked sadly at her. His hair had begun to disappear. So had Erika's. Luc then turned to go.

One by one the children returned to their wheelchairs and their beds. One by one, these little troopers put back on their braces and slings and scarves and eye patches and bandages.

Luc, too. He returned to his wheelchair again. He found himself losing his strength and then he was weak again. His hair was now completely gone again and the surgical scars on the top of his head had returned. He leaned over the edge of his chair, picked up his scarf from the ground where he had dropped it, and put it on.

Erika's hair was gone, too. She returned to her bed and found herself in the same position she had been in when the camp bell first began ringing. When she woke up she realized it had all been a wonderful dream. In her dream all of the wishes she had made on the night of the Perseids meteor shower had come true, for she had wished for each and every camp member to be healthy and happy.

On the last day of camp Erika and Luc were playing chess. They talked. Erika was telling him about Mrs. McGillacuddy. Luc was very tired; more so than on the day she had returned to camp.

"She said next time she'd call the dogcatcher. She upsets my parents. I'm so mad at her," Erika said.

Erika then made her move on the chessboard and waited for Luc to make his, but Luc didn't do anything. He sat there pondering what she had just told him.

"It's your move," she reminded him after a short while.

Luc took in a deep breath and look perplexed.

"What? What's wrong, Luc?" Erika asked. She was becoming worried.

"Ya know...sometimes...sometimes you have to be bold," he finally said with firmness. Ya just have to be bold."

"What do you mean?" Erika asked.

"Have fun while you can. Take a chance and do something that's big and dangerous. Who cares? Do something that'll get their attention. *That's* what I mean."

"I don't understand. What are you talking about?" Erika asked, puzzled.

Luc then spoke in a tone more fitting for a proclamation. "Time is too short and precious to waste on those useless emotions. Take anger, for example. You said you were 'mad' at her. Being angry is a waste of time. What good is it? What will it get you? Nothing! So why bother being angry at this rich, old hag?" Luc then stretched his arm skyward as though he were gripping Excalibur in his hand and yelled to the sky, "Viva today! Live each day to the fullest! There may not be many tomorrows!"

"Well, yeah," Erika agreed. "But I still don't know what to do about her."

"Ya know what you do? Make her see your point. Make a statement!"

"A 'statement'?"

"Yeah! Do something so outrageous that they'll never forget you after you're gone. That way you'll know your dog will be safe because they'll always remember you."

"I kind of understand what you mean, Luc. But I don't know what you mean," Erika admitted.

"You will. Just remember: Don't be afraid to be bold, Erika. Be bold and think big."

Luc then refocused his wandering attention on the chess. He made a move with his queen and then smiled at her.

"Checkmate," he said.

MRS. MCGILLACUDDY'S SINISTER PLOT!

Mooflee wiggled her way through the hole in the hedgerow in the backyard and walked up to the nice man. The nice man was holding a thick, juicy steak in his hand.

"Sit down, girl," he said.

Mooflee quickly obeyed. She was mesmerized by the sight and scent of the succulent piece of meat. Her mouth dripped with saliva and she had to lick her chops several times.

"Good girl," the man said. He reached out and petted Mooflee on the head.

Mooflee liked the man next door. He had been kind to her all throughout the summer. Every time he had whispered for her to come over to the hedgerow he had a special treat for her, just as he did now.

"Here ya go." He tossed the steak on the ground and watched the dog happily pounce on it.

Upstairs in the mansion, Mrs. McGillacuddy was opening the draperies in her bedroom. Her bedroom had a beautiful view overlooking the magnificent flower gardens on the grounds. As she pulled back the silk brocade, she was shocked by what she saw! There was her husband standing by the hedgerow feeding the neighbor's horrid sheepdog! She couldn't believe it! She was stunned! The rage in her rose so quickly she couldn't speak. Her face was red. Her hands began to shake! She was instantly furious at her husband for encouraging the dog onto her property and - worse yet! - for *feeding* him. She was just about to fling open the window and yell down at him to get that wretched animal out of her yard.

But then she stopped herself.

She suddenly was seized by an idea which she found much more appealing than yelling at her husband. Instead, she stepped back from the window and continued to watch her husband and the shaggy beast.

"I'll get rid of that dog," she said smugly to herself. "Once and for all."

Cecil McGillacuddy looked rather dapper as he climbed into his Rolls Convertible. He was dressed in a gray, pinstripe suit and wore wingtip shoes. His suit matched his short gray hair and he looked unusually business-like. Some of his friends and neighbors would not have recognized him from the drunken, big red-nosed, butterfly-chasing old man that was frequently seen dashing and staggering about, swinging a butterfly net around the huge estate's lawns. Nor would they have recognized his gait. This morning it was purposeful and had direction. Cecil McGillacuddy's brilliant red nose was not so brilliant on this particular morning. He had lightly powdered it to remove whatever sheen lingered. He climbed into his car and, without the aid of the chauffeur, drove off to his weekly country club luncheon in nearby Pittsford. He looked forward to these weekly meetings because nowadays they were practically his only opportunity to escape from his tyrannical wife and see his own friends.

"Enjoy your meeting, Cecil," Mrs. McGillacuddy said sweetly to her husband as he drove away. She even smiled and waved at him.

Cecil was taken aback by his wife's cheery mood and nearly lost control of his Rolls, running it off the pavement and almost hitting the large oak tree at the end of the driveway's loop. He spent the twenty-minute drive to Pittsford trying to figure out what had happened to put her in such an uncommon state.

After her husband had left, Mrs. McGillacuddy ran to the kitchen and pulled a thick steak from the freezer. She placed it in the microwave and thawed it. Minutes later, she placed it in a plastic sandwich bag and carried it out onto the terrace. It was a beautiful day and there was no one around. She casually strolled down the terrace steps and out into the gardens, pretending to take in the day. The whole time, however, the radar antennas in her head were turning and she was shooting glances through the hedgerow and then at the Reisling's backyard, looking for what she called the "giant furry beast." That was her name for Mooflee.

She wandered through her gardens, maneuvering closer and closer to the property line. She sneaked peaks through the openings in the hedgerow as she admired her garden. She did not want to be seen by any of the Reislings.

Finally, she saw it: the giant furry beast. It was lying in the middle of the Reisling's backyard quietly licking its paws.

Mrs. McGillacuddy walked closer to the hedgerow. She continued to look around and still saw no one. Standing at the exact spot where her husband had been standing, she could see a large, thin opening in the hedge. Looking through it, she had a good view of the Reisling's entire backyard. Satisfied there were no children or parents around, she whispered to the dog.

"Hey, you!"

When Mooflee didn't responded, Mrs. McGillacuddy made a peculiar clicking-sucking sound with her lips and then followed this odd noise with a "Psss."

Mooflee stopped her paw licking and looked up. She turned her big head this way and that, trying to located the source of the unusual sound.

Mrs. McGillacuddy repeated her sounds.

Curious, Mooflee stood up and began walking toward the hedgerow.

Mrs. McGillacuddy grinned as the dog approached.

Maybe the kind old man had returned with another treat, Mooflee thought. The dog couldn't really see very well. Her long, shaggy hair covered most of her cow eyes and all she mostly saw was white hair with bits and pieces of a moving picture on the other side of it. As long as she kept moving her head around, she could piece together enough of a picture of the real world to tell her what was going on around her.

She could see the hedgerow and a shape behind it, but it was the scent that first alerted her to the fact it was not the kind old man calling to her. It was the scent of the nasty old woman, instead; the one who had tried to whack her with the rake.

Mooflee stopped dead in her tracks.

Mrs. McGillacuddy's evil grin turned to a frown. "Come here, you!" she whispered harshly. "Why are you stopping?"

Mooflee stood there motionless, trying to figure out what the woman wanted.

"Come here, you dummy!" Mrs. McGillacuddy hissed again. "I've got something for you."

When that didn't work, Mrs. McGillacuddy opened the plastic sandwich bag. "Look what I have for you, 'Doggy.'"

The air carried the scent of the steak straight to Mooflee's nose. When it entered her nostrils, her fuzzy, floppy ears shot upward up like a pair of antennae. The smell was overwhelming and her mouth began to get juicy and she began to lick her chops again. It drove her nuts and she began walking toward the hedge again.

"That's a good doggy," Mrs. McGillacuddy said, grinning once again. "Keep coming."

Mooflee was blind with the desire to sink her teeth into the steak. She figured that maybe the nasty old woman had changed and was trying to be a *kind* old woman, like her husband; that the steak was like a peace offering.

With that dog rationale in mind, Mooflee cautiously crawled through the small opening in the hedge.

"Here you are," Mrs. McGillacuddy said as nice as pie as she took the steak out of the bag and held it in front of the dog.

Mooflee paused, but then bit the steak. It was wonderful! It was fantastic! Her taste buds exploded in ecstasy...but when she tried to pull the meat away, the old woman wouldn't let go.

"You mangy fur ball," Mrs. McGillacuddy said, her tone suddenly turning sinister. "You're trespassing."

Mooflee didn't understand what was going on. All she knew was she wanted to eat that steak and she pulled harder, but the old woman still wouldn't let go.

"You don't think I'm really going to give you this fine steak, do you, you skuzzy creature?" she sneered.

Mooflee wasn't listening. She was becoming annoyed at this silly game of tug of war. Not only that, but she couldn't see very well with all of her shaggy white hair in her eyes and so when she attempted to get a better jaw grip on the steak, she accidentally nipped Mrs. McGillacuddy's fingers in the process.

"Oww!" Mrs. McGillacuddy howled in pain as she let go of the steak. She looked at her hand. It was bleeding from two cuts.

"You bit me!" she yelled hysterically. "You bit me! Not only are you trespassing, but you bit me, too!"

Mooflee continued to ignore her and gobble down the steak.

Mrs. McGillacuddy calmed down and then smiled as she realized something else. "Ha! It's my lucky day!"

She went into her mansion and immediately called the sheriff.

Little did she know that little Johnny Ingle was hiding in the Reisling's tree house and had seen the whole thing.

MOOFLEE IS ARRESTED!

Erika stopped by Doc's house to deliver his mother's order of Girl Scout cookies.

While she was there, Doc took her downstairs to his lab where he demonstrated his latest invention. Inspired by Erika's story of the beach food fight at Peggy Winkleman's birthday party, Doc called it his "Smart Cake." He had imbedded a miniature CCD into, of all things, a Hostess Twinkie. He then hurled it at the basement wall. As with his bow and arrow demonstration with the *SS Enterprise* model, both the Twinkie and CCD components were destroyed after their brief flight through the air and into the wall.

"That's pretty neat, Doc, but I don't see any use for it," Erika said, shrugging her shoulders. "All you're doing is throwing away a perfectly good Twinkie; not to mention a TV chip every time you crash something. Plus, now you have a big mess to clean up."

Doc merely shrugged and replied, "It's something to do."

She then left Doc's basement and headed home.

When she returned home, Erika saw a sheriff's car and a van marked "Dogcatcher" pull up in front of her house. Standing at the corner of their property was Mrs. McGillacuddy.

Mooflee was laying in the front yard watching the world go by.

"That's the dog that bit me!" Mrs. McGillacuddy yelled at the sheriff's deputy. "See the marks on my hand? I was bleeding! It's dangerous. Be careful!"

The deputy walked to the front door of the Reisling's and knocked while the dogcatcher took Mooflee by the collar and began dragging her toward his van. Mooflee didn't understand what was going on. Erika was shocked.

"Hey! Where are you going with my dog?" Erika yelled as she ran after the man dragging her dog away. "Leave her alone! Let her go!" Erika grabbed Mooflee's collar and pulled, too, resulting in a tug of war with the dogcatcher. Mooflee was being yanked back and forth by the neck. She then decided she didn't like this game and began to growl at the dogcatcher.

"See?" Mrs. McGillacuddy shouted at the deputy. "She's a mad dog! Probably has rabies!"

"She is not, you old witch!" Erika shouted back

Just then Erika saw her mom open the front door. Mrs. Reisling was appalled when she saw the commotion going on in her front yard.

"What's going on here, Officer??" she demanded to know. "What are you doing with our dog?"

"Mom! Mom! Mrs. McGillacuddy is having Mooflee taken away!"

Mrs. Reisling quickly pushed open the screen door and stepped outside. She saw Mrs. McGillacuddy standing beside the sheriff's car in the street; a smug expression smeared across her face.

"Mrs. Reisling," the deputy began to explain, "we've had a complaint by your next door neighbor, Mrs. McGillacuddy over there, that she was attacked by your dog."

"If that's true, then Mrs. McGillacuddy no doubt prompted it herself. She's always hated our dog and has attempted to injure her many times in the past."

"Mrs. Reisling, the deputy continued, "she has a bite mark on her hand which she claims was inflicted by your dog. Also, she says your dog trespassed on her property and destroyed many of her flowers."

"Officer, that woman is lying. I want my dog released right now!" Mrs. Reisling demanded. She then yelled at Mrs. McGillacuddy who was clearly enjoying the moment. "How could you do this? What's wrong with you?"

"Your dog bit me!" Mrs. McGillacuddy yelled back, shaking her gauze-covered hand at them. She had wrapped her hand so many times with the white gauze that one would have thought her entire appendage had been completely ripped off during the skirmish with the sheepdog. As she spoke she waved the big wad of gauze on her hand around for emphasis.

"Mrs. Reisling, I'm sorry," the deputy apologized. "I can't release your dog. I have to do my job here and take the dog for now until the judge can decide whether she's dangerous or not."

The deputy then waved at the dogcatcher to go ahead. The dogcatcher nodded and with one last tug, he successfully broke Erika's grip on Mooflee's collar. As Mooflee whined and struggled, the dogcatcher then forcefully shoved Mooflee into the cage in the back of his van and quickly slammed the doors so the dog wouldn't escape. Mooflee barked and looked helplessly at Erika through the van's back window. The dogcatcher got in and then drove away.

"Give me back my dog!" Erika yelled as he drove away, tears running down her face.

"I'm sorry, Mrs. Reisling," the deputy said as he handed her a citation.

Erika then looked at Mrs. McGillacuddy who was still standing there enjoying the moment. Their eyes met and Mrs. McGillacuddy smiled smugly at her. Erika then began yelling at her.

"You're nothing but a ruthless witch, Mrs. McGillacuddy!"

"Erika, stop!" Mrs. Reisling said. "Let's go inside."

"What an undisciplined little brat, you have," Mrs. McGillacuddy quipped as she walked away.

"I just can not believe the arrogance of that woman," Mrs. Reisling said with great restraint as she took her daughter inside their home.

Just then the telephone rang. Mrs. Reisling answered it.

"Witch!" Erika shouted as she furiously stomped her foot on the kitchen floor.

Mrs. Reisling covered the phone and said, "Erika, quiet, please!"

Erika saw her mom with the telephone in her hand and quickly settled down. She then watched and listened.

"Hello!" Mrs. Reisling said angrily. "Yes, this is the Reisling residence. Speak up, please! This is Mrs. Reisling. Who is this?" After a moment Mrs. Reisling calmed down and said, "Oh, good afternoon, Mrs. Maille. I'm sorry. We're just having a moment of chaos here, that's all. How is Luc?"

It seemed to Erika that her mom's question took a lifetime to answer. She watched as her mom sat down on a chair. The expression of anger on her face disappeared and was replaced by one of sad concern. Mrs. Reisling looked at her daughter. She finally said in a cracked voice, "I'm so sorry, Mrs. Maille. I really am. Yes, I'll tell her."

Erika listened in disbelief. She did not need her mother to tell her what was said.

"Thank you for letting us know, Mrs. Maille. Au revoir."

THE CHESS TABLE

A few days later Erika asked her parents if she could spend the day at Camp Good Days. They said okay and dropped her off.

Mrs. Maille was in her cabin packing her things for the long trip back home to France when she noticed Erika walk by. She was heading for the lake.

Erika sat at the chess table alone, toying with the chess pieces while staring out at the tranquility of the lake. It was odd Luc wasn't there. His seat at the chessboard was empty. She glanced around the camp behind her and looked at all of the happy children playing different games and engaged in different activities. Perhaps Luc was really there, playing among them.

"Erika..." a familiar voice said. It was Marina. She walked up to the grieving child and stared out at the lake with her.

"Hi, Marina," Erika said.

"Hello," the counselor said. She sat down. "Pretty quiet out here at the chess table. You two were among the few who used it."

"Why did he have to go, Marina?"

Marina said softly, "I don't know, Sweetie. These things just happen without reason. We just accept them and move on."

Erika continued to stare out at the lake as she touched the chess pieces. "'For many a flower's born to blush unseen and waste its sweetness on the desert air,'" she said.

"That's beautiful," Marina added.

"It's not mine. It's a quotation from someone important."

"It's still beautiful," Marina added.

"Erika," another voice said.

Erika turned and saw Mrs. Maille standing there.

Marina stood, patted Erika on the shoulder, and left the two women alone.

"Mrs. Maille, I'm so sorry."

"Merci. Thank you."

Mrs. Maille was sad, but she seemed to be at peace with herself. Erika noticed her nervous and high-strung manner was no longer present. Instead, Mrs. Maille was calm. She sat down in Luc's place and took a moment to look out over the lake.

Struggling with her English, she said, "I saw you walk by my cabin. Here...Luc, he told me to give this to Erika. To you."

She held out her hand. In it was a chess piece. It was the queen that Luc had last checkmated her with.

Erika smiled. She reached across the table and took it.

"Thank you, Mrs. Maille," Erika said as her eyes studied the piece.

"You made him happy here," Mrs. Maille said. Her eyes began to swell with tears. "I am very grateful to you. Merci." She began to cry.

Erika rose from her chair, walked around the table, and gave Mrs. Maille a hug.

"We'll all miss him, Mrs. Maille."

The happy children behind them continued to play.

THE PLAN

Erika sat in the living room of her home as she fidgeted with the chess piece that Luc had left her.

It was a gloomy, dreary day as rain poured down on the Reisling house. An occasional rumble of thunder could be heard in the distance. Inside where it was dry and warm, Erika, Melanie, Jo, and Doc were playing *Monopoly*. The television was on in the background and a *Three Stooges* episode was in progress.

Michele was sitting at the piano practicing her scales. Her playing was annoying Erika.

"Michele, please stop," Erika said. "We're trying to talk."

Michele said, "I have to practice, Erika. My lesson is this afternoon."

Erika said, "Practice later. Watch TV for a while. Please?"

"All right," Michele said, and she stopped practicing. "I miss Mooflee."

"I do, too, Michele. Don't worry. She'll be back soon," Erika told her.

"When?"

"I don't know when. But we'll get her back soon," Erika assured her. There was frustration in her voice. She really didn't know when.

Michele sat down in front of the television just as the *Stooges* launched into another one of their countless pie fights. Michele laughed as she watched the snobbish aristocrats getting hit in the face with cream pies.

Doc said, "What a witch she is for having Mooflee taken away."

"You can say that again," Melanie agreed.

"You know, there's got to be something you can do, Erika," Doc continued. "Listen, I heard she's having this big deal garden party real soon. It's in honor of Senator Clydesdale who shows up once in a blue moon for the occasion. He's running for President this year and so he is definitely coming. He's looking for the 'big bucks' to fund his campaign. The 'Dread goes gaga over him and loves to be seen with him. A lot of important people are coming just because he's a Presidential candidate."

"Maybe you can ask the Senator for help," Jo suggested. "Senators are supposed to help people, right?"

"Yeah," Doc said. "Maybe if you wrote him it might do the trick."

Erika asked, "Doc, how do you know Mrs. M is having a big party?"

Doc's mischievous smile appeared. "I was toying with my phone scanner and I 'accidentally' listened in to the 'Dread's cordless calls. Piece of cake."

"They won't give you a 'lobotomy' over that, will they?" Jo asked.

"Oh, no. Anyone can buy a scanner and listen to cordless phones," Doc answered. "Listen, Erika, the party's going to be an expensive, invitation-only affair. She wouldn't look good in front of her friends if they knew she had thrown Mooflee in doggy jail."

"Contacting the Senator might be a good idea, Erika," Melanie said.

"A big party. Hmm," Erika said.

As she stared at the game board, Erika thought of Luc and heard his voice.

"Sometimes you have to be bold. Take a chance and do something that's big and dangerous."

"Hmm. Maybe there's something else I can do," Erika said.

"If there is, I'd like to know what," Doc said.

Luc spoke again. *"Who cares? Do something that'll get their attention!"*

"What do you think?" Jo asked.

"Write the Senator?" Doc added. "Better yet, let's call his office!"

"Time is too short and precious to waste."

Erika said, "We have to do...something."

Melanie said, "Yes, Erika. We know, but what?"

"Make her see your point. Make a statement!"

Michele laughed out loud as she watched her show.

"Michele, what's so funny over there?" Erika asked as she glanced at the television to see what her sister was watching.

"This show is so silly," Michele said as she giggled.

Erika saw the *Stooges* were in the middle of a heated pie fight. She continued to stare at the screen several long moments.

"You know what you do? Do something that'll get their attention!"

Erika smiled as Curly was splattered in the face with a cream pie. Her smile widened as an idea climbed into her head and quickly found a home.

"We'll disrupt her garden party," Erika said firmly to her friends. "That's what we'll do." She left the others at the game board and sat on the couch beside her sister to watch. Michele's laughter erupted again as a debutante got creamed in the face with another flying pie.

"Disrupt her garden party?" Doc questioned.

"How?" Jo wanted to know.

Melanie said, "We could stand at the hedgerow and make faces at the people."

Doc said, "What kind of an idea is that? We'd be the ones who would look stupid if we did that."

When Erika didn't answer, the kids turned their attention to the television. One by one, they all watched with interest. One by one, they laughed as one adult after another had their fine, Sunday-best clothes splattered by flying cream pies. One by one, Erika's friends began to suspect what was going on inside of Erika's mind.

Erika looked at her friends and gave them a knowing smile.

Looking at the TV set, she said, "*This* is what we do."

89

"Viva today! Live each day at a time to the fullest! There may not be many tomorrows!"

ERIKA AND VICTORIA UNITE!

Big plans need lots of help and Erika was not one to let petty rivalries get in the way when it came to asking for it. She, Melanie, and Jo bicycled to Victoria's secret clubhouse to ask for her assistance in the plan.

Erika was feeling nauseous after the previous day's chemotherapy. No sooner had they arrived and Victoria and her group of friends came out, when Erika threw up in the bushes.

The other kids were grossed out.

"What's wrong with you?" Victoria asked snottily.

"Nothing," Erika said as she composed herself. "Victoria, I need your help. Mrs. McGillacuddy had our dog impounded."

"I heard about that from Anna. What a witch she is. All I can say is I wish there was something we could do about it."

"There is," Erika said. A second later she turned and threw up again.

"Erika!" Melanie cried out with concern. "Are you all right?"

"Just an upset stomach," Erika responded, attempting to compose herself again.

"Gross. You look awful, Reisling," Victoria observed. "Geez, always looking for sympathy."

Angered, Erika strutted right up to Victoria, stopping only inches from her face.

"Hey, don't throw up on me!" Victoria said, taking two steps backwards.

Erika shouted, "You think I throw up for *sympathy*? Don't you understand anything, Victoria? I've been dealing with this illness for nearly a year now and you *still* don't get it? I can't do anything about my disease, or how I appear," she said snatching the baseball cap off her bald head. I didn't choose to have this disease. It's not my choice. It's not fun for me. It's not fun for my family. I'm just grateful none of my friends have it. Including an idiot like you!"

Victoria was speechless. She suddenly felt guilty about the way she had been treating Erika over the year. "I'm sorry, Erika. I...I heard about your friend in camp. Anna told me that, too. I'm sorry your friend died," Victoria said. "I'm sorry I've been mean to you."

Erika studied Victoria's face for a moment and knew she was telling the truth. She said, "I never took it seriously, Victoria. I just thought you were too dumb to know any better."

"I guess I was," Victoria admitted. "But when I heard about your friend... Well, I'm sorry."

"It's okay," Erika said, a small smile of appreciation breaking across her face.

"So, what can we do about your dog?" Victoria asked.

"We're going to attack Mrs. M's garden party this Saturday on bicycles."

"You're what?!" Victoria asked incredulously.

"We're going to spoil her garden party."

"Awesome," Victoria said, looking at her friends. "How?"

"We have a plan. It's called 'Plan Nine from Outer Space'," Erika announced. They all gave Erika a funny look.

"'Plan Nine from Outer Space'?" Victoria asked. "What does that mean?"

"It's a code-name so no one will know what we're doing. It comes from a famous bad movie somebody once made. I saw it at camp a few weeks ago. A good friend of mine at camp told me about it," Erika said, thinking of Marvin.

Victoria glanced skeptically at Toni and Kasey "So what is 'Plan 9'?" she asked.

"It's simple," Erika's said enthusiastically. "We're going to disrupt the 'Dread's next garden party and *make* her give us Mooflee back at all costs!"

"Wow! What a bold idea!" Victoria exclaimed.

MOOFLEE IN JAIL

Mooflee was terribly sad. She missed her nice home and family. Instead, she found herself behind bars in the basement section of the dog pound. It was lonely and dingy down there. It was dark and the old, stone walls were damp. Water pipes next to her cage were leaking and occasionally rattled. There were cobwebs and spiders in the ceiling overhead, as well. There were several other dogs in the section of the pound where she was located, but because it was so dark she couldn't see many of them. For all Mooflee knew there might have been a cage full of alligators on the other side of the room.

Just then she heard the sound of a door opening echo from down the hall. It was steel and heavy; the hinges screeched loudly, hurting her ears to the point where she let out a small whine. A light clicked on. Mooflee shook her head to throw some of her hair out of her eyes so she could see what was happening. Looking down the hall, she recognized the grizzly pound keeper who had locked her up in her jail cell after the dogcatcher dropped her off. The pound keeper had been gruff and uncaring, and now he was back and approaching her cage. She thought maybe he had come to release her. The pound keeper, however, went to the cage next to her's and opened that door. The cocker spaniel in that cage began moaning, scared of what this jail-keep was preparing to do. The pound keeper grabbed the dog by his collar and dragged him out of the cage. The dog locked all four of his paws, not wanting to go, but the pound keeper easily overpowered him and yanked him from the cage. The dog began whining so loud that one would think he was going to be X-ed in front of a firing squad. But then, a little girl appeared at the end of the hall, followed by her mother, father, and brother. The pound keeper released the dog and it quickly ran to its family. It was happy to see them and gave them all licks.

Mooflee watched the happy little girl and grateful family leave. She then thought about her own family: Erika and Michele; Mom and Dad. She missed them all and wished they would come for her.

As if her doggy wish had been answered at that very instant, Mooflee thought she heard Erika's voice. Her furry ears perked.

The happy family and their dog were leaving the pound just as Erika and Michele arrived. With keys in hand, the pound keeper held the door open for the departing family. As soon as they were out, he closed it and was about to lock it.

"Wait!" Erika said loudly as she and her sister hurried to the door.

The pound keeper opened the door again and asked, "What do you want, kids?"

"I'm Erika Reisling."

"I'm Michele."

"So?" he asked.

"My sheepdog is here," Erika continued. "May I see her, please?"

"The sheepdog, huh?"

"Yes, sir," Erika answered.

"Hmm." The pound keeper glanced at his watch and barked, "It's a little late in the day, isn't it, young lady? It's just about quitting time. Time for me to lock up the place and go home."

"Oh, please, sir. I'm sorry to inconvenience you, but we haven't seen our dog in days. Please let us in; just for a few minutes," she begged.

"Yeah. Please?" Michele added. "We really miss our dog, Mister. Can we see her?"

"I want to make sure she's okay," Erika said.

The pound keeper frowned and grumbled something unintelligible to himself. After a moment he said, "Oh, all right. Just for a minute. But that's all! I'm in a hurry."

"Thank you, sir," Erika said.

"Follow me," he grunted.

He led the two girls down into the basement and took out his jingling keys. He unlocked the door to the cage area and shoved it open. The girls grimaced as the huge hinges screeched.

Clicking on the light switch, the pound keeper said blandly, "Turn right. Her cage is at the end."

The girls entered the cage area. Once inside, the pound keeper closed the door behind them and left. Mooflee began barking right away as the heavy door slammed.

Erika and Michele looked at each other with apprehension. It was a spooky place and they were a little frightened as they looked down the darkened corridor, but they were happy to see Mooflee at the end of the long row of mostly empty cages.

"Erika, this place is yucky," Michele said as she looked up and down the filthy walls and the pipe-laden ceiling.

"It looks like a dungeon in here," her sister commented as she led Michele towards Mooflee's dark cage.

"Hi, Mooflee," both girls said.

Mooflee was excited to see her best friends. Erika and Michele approached the cage and stuck their fingers through the bars to try to pet her. Mooflee eagerly licked them.

Erika looked with disgust at the grim condition that surrounded her dog. "Don't worry, Mooflee. We'll get you out of this dreadful place as soon as we can," Erika promised. She noticed how scared her dog appeared to be.

"Yeah, Mooflee, don't be sad," Michele said, touching Mooflee's hair through the cage.

"If only you could tell us what happened between you and Mrs. McGillacuddy," Erika said.

"Too bad dogs can't talk," Michele added.

Just then the heavy door opened again. The pound keeper had returned.

"Time's up, little girls. Let's go. I don't want to miss one second of the Bills' game."

Erika and Michele looked sadly at Mooflee and bid her good-bye.

"We'll be back," Erika said to the dog.

Mooflee whined as she watched her best friends leave. She couldn't understand why she couldn't go with them. She began barking and jumping up on the cage door.

"So, you're the owners of the dog that bit Mildred McGillacuddy?" the pound keeper asked, chuckling, as Erika and Michele went upstairs. "Good luck ever seeing that animal again. It'll probably be locked away in here forever."

The grizzly man clicked off the light and grunted as he closed the heavy, steel door. He then locked it. Mooflee continued to bark from within.

"Please be gentle with our dog, Mister," Erika said. "She's not used to being in a dog pound."

"Who is?" the pound keeper asked with sarcasm. "All of the dogs hate it here. I don't have a clue why."

"Mister, is it possible for her to be placed in a better cage?" Erika ventured.

The pound keeper gave Erika and Michele a dirty look. "No. That's not possible at all because what you saw in there is the best we have."

"Well, thank you," Erika said with disappointment. "Come on, Michele. Let's go home." She led Michele towards the front door.

The pound keeper added, "I'll tell you one thing: I'll be glad when the judge decides what to do with your dog."

"Why's that?" Erika asked.

"She makes too much noise. How do you get that dog to shut-up?"

Erika looked the pound keeper in the eye and answered, "Let her out of the dog pound."

"Smart aleck," he said and locked the door behind them.

Though they were distressed because they couldn't take their dog with them, Erika and Michele knew Mooflee was basically all right - for now. After seeing the squalid conditions that the sheepdog was now living in, Erika was more determined than ever to go through with *Plan 9*.

MIL-DREAD'S DAY!

The elegantly dressed guests began arriving at the McGillacuddy estate shortly before noon. Nearly two hundred were expected. Most were coming from Rochester and Canandaigua, though some were coming from as far away as Buffalo and Albany. The caterer and his staff were busy preparing and serving food. It was a very hot day and the bartender and his staff were busy making drinks for all of the thirsty guests that crowded around his long table. A lovely soloist accompanied by a string quartet was singing on the deck. The tuxedo-dressed quartet consisted of a harp, cello, and two violins. Given the backdrop of the famous McGillacuddy gardens, the event with its beauty and sounds was truly a wondrous sight to behold.

People were people, however, and no matter where you found them, they consisted of all types. A couple of gossipy women made fun of another woman who walked by. A businessman was overheard bragging about his closing a deal that had resulted in the ripping-off of one of the other party guests. Another guest, a Mr. Carlton, had consumed too much alcohol *before* the party and was busily engaged in bragging to a couple of ladies about his last African safari.

"I just returned from safari in Africa. I was in Kenya. Hot place, Kenya. The place was literally overflowing with lions," he blustered.

The two women, dressed in formal attire, listened with interest as the imbibed guest boasted of his adventures.

Erika, Yancy, Doc, and others, including Anna and Peggy, were all stationed at various locations, awaiting the arrival of Senator Clydesdale. Before they put Plan 9 into operation, they wanted to make sure he was there. With a walkie-talkie in her pocket, Erika waited for word at Victoria's secret clubhouse while Doc watched the street for the Senator's limousine.

Yancy was spending the week with the Reislings after Erika invited her to come. She was happy to be a part of Plan 9.

"This should be as much fun as Camp Good Days," Yancy said excitedly when she heard the grand plan. "I wouldn't miss it for the world."

Erika was ecstatic to have her new friend there.

Mrs. McGillacuddy stepped out onto her deck and fanned herself. She surveyed her guests amongst her gardens. Most were leaders in business, politics, and entertainment. There was no other person there who was as wealthy as she and this made her feel important and powerful, for they were there at her house because of her and *only* her. The arrival of Senator Clydesdale, once again, would prove to the world her importance, just as she thought it did every year; only more so this year, for Senator Clydesdale was a now Presidential candidate.

As Mrs. McGillacuddy stood there gloating over her own self-importance, the lovely soloist spoke to her as the quartet continued to play only a few feet away.

"Mrs. McGillacuddy...ah, we've been playing for two hours," the young woman said. "I know we didn't discuss it, but could we take a brief ten-minute break?"

"There's a reason we didn't discuss it, my dear," Mrs. McGillacuddy began pleasantly, at first. Turning curt, she continued, "I'm not paying you to take a break. I'm paying all of you to sing and to play! You can take a break *after* the garden party is over. And don't stop singing or playing until I tell you otherwise. Do I make myself clear?"

"Yes, Ma'am, Mrs. McGillacuddy," the soloist obeyed, and returned to the quartet.

"Cecil!" Mrs. McGillacuddy bellowed to her husband.

Senator Clydesdale arrived in his fat, stretch limousine followed by several nondescript cars carrying Secret Service agents. The limo just barely made it around the corner without scraping against a tree. The Senator climbed out, exchanged greetings, and then joined the party of merrymakers. Secret Service agents wearing sunglasses fanned out, but stayed close to him, looking for any would-be assailants hiding in the thin Canandaigua underbrush. As the Senator made his way through the crowd of gathered distinguished guests, a local newspaper reporter approached him. The reporter was doing a story on Senator Clydesdale's visit to Canandaigua and was busy taking pictures of the elegant affair and its guests with the Nikon that was hanging around his neck.

"Senator, may I have a picture, please?" the reporter asked.

The Senator, seeing the photo op, nodded. He stopped momentarily, smiled for the camera, and the picture was snapped. He then continued working his way through the crowd.

Doc picked up his radio. "Erika...he's here."

It was time. Erika and her friends mounted their bicycles. As she did, she suddenly began to feel weak and tired. She winced briefly in pain and felt nauseous.

She heard Luc's voice again. *"Viva today! Live each day at a time to the fullest! There may not be many tomorrows!"*

The spell passed and Erika shoved off on her bicycle with Yancy, Melanie, Jo, and the others behind her.

They rendezvoused with Doc and his friends, and Victoria and her friends out in the street in front of the McGillacuddy mansion. There were nearly twenty children in total on bicycles. They had baskets lashed to their handlebars or they were wearing backpacks, all of which were loaded with organic ammunition of various sorts.

All of the children waited for Erika's signal. Erika looked at all of her friends who had come to her aid to help her get her dog back. She was so proud and felt so warm that all of her friends had turned out to help her. She looked with pride at Yancy, Melanie, and then Jo, Doc, and Victoria. There were several other kids she didn't even know, but who had come to help free Mooflee. Both Erika and Victoria smiled at each other. She then looked at Doc who was sitting on his bike, which was a bizarre contraption to say the least. It was rigged with all types of high tech gear and antennas.

Victoria looked at Erika and said, "We're ready whenever you are, Erika."

Erika nodded to Victoria, and then to all of them she yelled, "Let's do it! VIVA TODAY!"

Erika then led the charge! She could hear a loud cheer rise from behind her as she wheeled her bicycle around and headed up the McGillacuddy's driveway. All of the children began pumping their pedals as hard as they could and they proceeded toward the house. The Secret Service agents who were stationed in the front yard didn't know what to make of this motley group of kids on bicycles. They were surprised when they saw the children coming, but there were too many of them to stop. They tried to grab some of the kids, but were out maneuvered and the kids narrowly slipped their grasp.

When the children reached the head of the McGillacuddy's driveway, they drove onto the grounds and out back toward the gardens and to the party. One of the Secret Service agents saw Erika and her friends streaming in from around the corner of the house, but was too late to stop them. Erika tossed the first Twinkie and from that moment on there was utter chaos. She didn't throw it at anyone in particular, but simply threw it hard and fast into the crowd. The cupcake arched through the air, missed a half-dozen guests, and then slammed into shoulder of a world famous actress. The person the actress was talking to couldn't control her surprise and started laughing out loud.

All of the children then began lobbing food into the air, hitting guests at random. Victoria and her friends split off from the main force and began reeking havoc in another section of the party. Bikes were suddenly appearing up and down the stone walkways in between the gardens. The children were tossing tomatoes, eggs, and Twinkies left and right.

Many of the two hundred guests had not seen the children arrive and had no idea of what was going on. Guests were getting hit with flying food which seemed to come out of nowhere. Some of those guests became angry and picked up something and threw it at someone else.

Doc had pretty much emptied the produce section of his mother's refrigerator into his backpack. He was flinging anything he could get his hands on in quick, rapid-fire order. He was whipping tomatoes, eggs, mushrooms, and even celery sticks as quickly as he could pull them out of his backpack. Food was falling out of the sky! At one point he stopped his bike and pulled out one of his Smart Cakes. The antenna on his bike whipped wildly forward as he came to a screeching stop. He turned on the Sony Watchman strapped to his handlebar, pressed the record button, and then threw one of his Smart Cakes high into the air. In Doc's cellar video tape recorders were recording the transmissions from the cakes. Doc then watched on his bike screen as it descended upon a woman who had just thrown a Triscuit with herb dip at someone else. Just before the moment of impact she looked up to see the cake zeroing in on her face. The last thing Doc saw before the picture went dead was the woman's horrified face, mouth open.

"Big splat!" he said proudly. "Yes!"

Shortly after Erika's arrival and the food began flying, Senator Clydesdale was answering a few questions for the local newspaper reporter. The reporter listened with interest as he scribbled words onto his note pad. As the Senator elaborated about the need for a tougher crime bill in the state, he was suddenly hit in the face with a tomato. The stunned reporter turned to see where the tomato had come from. As soon as he turned, the lens on his Nikon was hit with a Twinkie and the hat on his head was knocked off by a cupcake. His note pad was splattered by the airborne contents of a glass of champagne punch that flew by overhead.

The children had initiated the attack, but it wasn't long before the adults perpetuated the fighting among themselves. The chain reaction had begun. Many of the guests still had not seen the children arrive and had merely thought one of the other guests had thrown the food at them. Those who were laughing were mistakenly taken to be the culprits and they, in turn, had food thrown at them. The chain reaction spread and continued!

The soloist and the string quartet members got slammed with cupcakes and spinach-artichoke dip, but the soloist did not stop singing nor did the quartet stop playing. Thinking the food fight that had erupted in front of them was some sort of weird, planned event that only rich people would dream up, they heeded Mrs. McGillacuddy's stern warning about not taking a break and they kept performing out of fear of not being paid. The harp's strings were getting covered with cake and dip while the quartet members dodged flying debris and cocktails. Doc lobbed a Smart Cake at the group and hit the cello player in the mouth.

"Bingo! Holy cello, Batman!" Doc said as he watched the event on his handle bar mounted TV monitor. "I love video!"

The bartender kept getting hit in the face with food as well. The caterer who was standing nearby, laughed out loud. Furious, the bartender picked up a bottle of seltzer and shot a pressurized stream of water into the man's cackling face.

The drunken Mr. Carlton continued to brag to the two women about his heroics during his trip to Kenya despite the commotion that was developing behind them. His two-lady audience continued to listen.

"And then - suddenly - there before me, was a lion the size of which I had never seen before! He began to charge at me and so I raised my rifle to fire!"

At that moment he was grazed across the forehead by a flying piece of cake. It left a trail of icing that resembled the tail of a comet. Carlton thought it was only a fly and he waved his hand to swat it away. His two lady friends were stunned, but Carlton did not notice and he continued on with his story.

"And *then* I heard a roar and I turned around. There was *another* lion behind me! This one was bigger than the first! I was trapped! So I swung my rifle around and fired both barrels!"

Just then a piece of chocolate cake followed by two eggs slammed into the side of his face and splattered on both women's expensive dresses. Both women gasped.

"Gosh, the bugs in the McGillacuddy's garden are atrocious! The flies here are as big as the ones in Africa," Mr. Carlton noted. "She should get out the bug spray! Anyway, as I was saying..."

SPLAT! Another flying piece of cake smacked him straight in the face, knocking him backwards, where he fell into the garden and flattened three-dozen rare white roses. That ended his safari story. Mortified, the two women fled.

In another section of the party, the world famous actress was wiping the icing off her face while the woman beside her continued to laugh at her.

The woman cackled, "So that's what you look like when you're offscreen. Who would have ever known?" and she continued to laugh.

The angered actress said, "Here's one thing I learned in the movies!" She picked up an apple torte from the dessert table and tossed it directly at the woman's face, but the woman quickly dodged it and the torte splattered into the woman standing directly behind her. The first lady roared with laughter, until both the actress and the other lady grabbed a couple of cake slices and then hit her so hard that she fell over backwards into the garden and destroyed more extraordinary plants.

Next door in the Reisling backyard, Michele and little Johnny Ingle were playing in the tree house when they heard the commotion over at the McGillacuddy's. Looking out the tree house door, they couldn't believe their eyes when they saw what was happening on the other side of the hedgerow. They saw bicycles zooming through the stone garden paths, adults throwing food, people yelling, laughing, and screaming, and fancy music playing in the background throughout.

"Wow! Look at that!" little Johnny exclaimed.

"Hey! There's my sister!" Michele shrieked.

"Come on, Michele. Let's go! I want to be a part of this!"

"Yeah! Me, too!"

Both children hurried down the makeshift tree house steps and ran toward the hedgerow.

Erika and her friends had begun a chain reaction that escalated beyond their wildest dreams. It was like watching a fire at a fireworks factory. People had no idea who started it, but they *darn well!* wanted to get even with those who messed up their expensive finery, hairdos, and makeup.

The person who took first prize for hitting Mrs. McGillacuddy in the face with a Hostess Cupcake was none other than Yancy. She had lobbed it high and far and it streaked downward, exploding directly onto Mrs. McGillacuddy's nose and face.

Mrs. McGillacuddy was so stunned, she could not speak.

Happy with her shot, Yancy quipped, "She's the hostess with the mostest Hostess!"

The cake on Mrs. M's face didn't last long for it was wiped off by a side-veering, horizontal-streaking tomato which hit and splattered on her left cheek and washed her face clean of the cupcake. It even took off half of her makeup. The remnants of the tomato flew directly into Senator Clydesdale's left ear.

Finding her voice buried deep within a face of cake remnants and tomato pulp, Mrs. McGillacuddy began shrieking. "Stop it! Stop it! All of you!" she yelled to her guests. "This is outrageous! STOP IT NOW!"

Her cries for order in her own backyard were instantly answered. She was hit in the face and shoulder with eggs, tortes, and Twinkies. Some irate guests tossed a couple of cocktails at her for good measure.

As Erika watched from the gardens, she was stopped dead in her bicycle tracks by the Secret Service agent who had seen her lead the charge. The agent had a Twinkie stuck on the top of his bald head. He pulled her from her bike.

The food fight that had erupted amongst the adults was now over. After the last cupcake and eggshell had splattered, the soloist and string quartet were still playing. Wiping the frosting and tomato juice from her face, Mrs. McGillacuddy turned abruptly to them and sharply said, "Oh, shut up!!"

Erika was taken to both the Senator and Mrs. McGillacuddy who were now standing together on her deck, trying to restore order. Cecil McGillacuddy was behind his wife wiping off his face. They were all covered with vegetables, frosting, and raspberry curd. Erika knew she was in big trouble now as she approached her nemesis. The other kids were caught as well, but Erika was singled out.

"We've caught the apparent 'ringleader' Senator," the agent said.

"Really?" the Senator said with restraint as he lay eyes upon the little girl. To the agent, he said, "Get that Twinkie off your head, Barnaby. You look silly."

"Yes, sir," the agent responded, and quickly shoved the cake off his head.

"I hate that kid," Mrs. McGillacuddy said as Erika was brought to her.

Erika heard Luc's voice again. *"Be bold. Make her see your point. Make a statement!"*

"Why did you do it, Erika Reisling?" Cecil McGillacuddy asked angrily.

"Because Mrs. McGillacuddy had Mooflee taken away."

"Taken away?" Cecil McGillacuddy was surprised. "What do you mean 'taken away'? That nice Old English sheepdog?" It was the first time he had heard about this.

"Your wife called the dogcatcher and had Mooflee taken to the pound."

Senator Clydesdale raised an eyebrow and looked at Mrs. McGillacuddy.

"Mildred? Is this true," Cecil asked.

"Yes, Mildred, is this true?" Senator Clydesdale asked with curiosity as he wiped a Hostess Cupcake from his face and excavated the remains of the tomato out of his left ear.

"Well, Senator," Mrs. McGillacuddy laughed, "Surely you don't believe these wretched brats?"

Erika shouted, "She did do it! Just ask my parents."

Cecil was incredulous for the first time in his life. "Mildred, is their dog in the pound?"

"Yes," Mrs. McGillacuddy answered with disgust. "Horrible creature."

Senator Clydesdale was suddenly not happy with Mildred McGillacuddy. "Why did you do this, Mildred? I'm an avid dog lover. I'm just nuts about them. Did the dog attack you?" he asked.

Erika interjected. "Mooflee's the kindest, most gentle dog in the whole world. She wouldn't hurt anybody!"

"It bit me!" Mrs. McGillacuddy hissed. "It kept coming into the yard and digging up my garden."

"She gave her a steak and then tried to pull it out of her mouth!" a faint voice was heard.

Several people looked around for the owner of the faint voice.

Out of the crowd stepped little Johnny Ingle. He was followed by Michele. Both children were covered from head to toe with icing and cake, especially in the area around their mouths. He marched through the crowd of towering adults and walked up to Senator Clydesdale.

"She gave her a steak!" he repeated.

Senator Clydesdale didn't see him or hear him, at first, so little Johnny began tugging on the Senator's pant leg to get his attention. "Hey, Mister! She gave her the steak."

The Senator finally looked down and saw the youngster. "What's that, little boy?"

"She gave her a steak and then tried to pull it out of her mouth!" little Johnny repeated, shouting. "When she did that, Mooflee accidently nipped her."

"Mrs. McGillacuddy?" the Senator asked the little boy.

Little Johnny answered empathically, "Yes!"

"How do you know this?" the Senator asked.

Johnny's little voice continued to shout. "I was hiding in the tree house that day and saw the whole thing!"

There was suddenly a murmur throughout the crowd. Everyone's eyes were on little Johnny, and then they shifted to Mrs. McGillacuddy.

Cecil McGillacuddy was the first to speak. "You *intentionally* lured the dog in, just so you could call the sheriff and have their dog taken away?" he demanded to know.

The 'Dread was seething with frustration, and yet she was speechless.

"She tried to hit Mooflee with a rake, too," Erika added.

Senator Clydesdale was so stunned he gasped. "Mildred, I'm shocked!"

Cecil looked down on his wife for the first time in years, if ever. "Mildred, how could you do such a thing to that nice dog and this little girl?"

"I warned them to keep their animal off my property," she said sternly.

"The dog was coming over here because *I* was feeding him," Cecil confessed.

"Feeding him? Why did you feed him??" Mrs. McGillacuddy demanded.

"I liked the sheepdog. I've always wanted one," Cecil said.

"That mangy creature...giving it our finest steaks!" Mrs. McGillacuddy snapped.

"That's the last straw." Cecil reached for the nearest piece of pastry he could find and planted it squarely in his wife's face. "Eat that, Mildred! You're despicable. That action is the lowest thing you've ever done. I've had it! I'm leaving you."

"Cecil!!" Mrs. McGillacuddy was stunned by her husband's reaction. When she scrapped the chocolate icing out of her eyes, she then noticed her friends were looking at her with contempt. There was another quiet murmur amongst her guests. Gradually there was distance in their eyes and, one by one, they began to walk away from her. "Cecil! Wait...!" she called again.

Senator Clydesdale was greatly disappointed. He said, "Mildred, I did not know you could be so cruel as to have a child's dog taken away."

"But, Senator...," she cowered.

"I'm really disappointed in you, Mildred," the Senator admonished.

Erika's parents arrived just then. They had heard the raucous from next door and came over to investigate. They were stunned as they surveyed the mess that surrounded them.

"Erika? Michele? What's going on here?" Mr. Reisling asked.

"Why are you over here?" Mrs. Reisling asked her daughters, and then noticed the gardens. They were a shambles. "Mrs. McGillacuddy...your gardens. What happened to your gardens?"

Mrs. McGillacuddy's fiery spirit had been crushed. Her voice was weak when she answered, "Your daughter and her friends..." She left the sentence dangling.

Cecil returned to help Erika.

Stunned, the Reislings looked at their daughter in disbelief. Gazing at the mess and destruction all around them, they asked, "Erika? You did *this*??"

Cecil smiled. He placed his arm on Erika's shoulder and said, "Don't worry about it, Mr. and Mrs. Reisling. Call it one, big accident. Erika did nothing that any other normal child would have done if their dog had been taken away."

Senator Clydesdale turned to Mrs. McGillacuddy and asked, "Why'd you do it, Mildred?"

She could not meet the Senator's harsh gaze. "I...I don't, ah. When I was a little girl...I, ah..."

Mrs. McGillacuddy suddenly couldn't speak. She took a deep breath as though she were about to say something harsh, but then contained it. She then held her head high, turned, and walked quickly to the safety of her cold, lonely mansion.

"I want the girl's dog released," the Senator said to Cecil.

Cecil responded, "Senator, I'll help Ms. Reisling get her dog out of the pound right away. Don't worry, Sir."

"Very well, then." Senator Clydesdale, still wiping the cake off his new suit, said to his Secret Service entourage, "Gentlemen, round up everyone and let's go. The garden party's over." Senator Clydesdale then turned to Erika. He knelt down so he could be on an even level with the little girl. Noting her hairless head, he realized she was undergoing treatment for something. He said, "Erika, you're a brave little girl to stand up to Mildred McGillacuddy like that. It takes guts to stand up for what you believe in. It takes guts to stand up to an injustice. I respect that in a person. But...in the future, just remember, that in our democracy even we in the Senate and those in the House of Representatives don't always throw Twinkies at each other whenever we want to get our way. That doesn't always work."

"Yes, sir," Erika acknowledged, a little embarrassed at the trouble she had caused. "I'll remember."

The Senator then added with a wink and a smile, "It did work this time, though."

"Yes, sir," Erika smiled back and agreed.

"I would very much like to meet your Mooflee sometime," the Senator continued. "The next time I'm in town I'd like to stop by your house - if it's all right with your parents - and visit you both."

Erika glanced up at her parents, who both nodded that it was okay. "That would be great, Senator."

"Okay, then," he said taking her hand and shaking it. He then stood up and left with his entourage following close behind him.

By now most of the guests had gone and the few people that remained were the food servers.

Cecil shook his head and then said, "Come on, then, Erika. Let's go to the pound and get that pup released." To Mr. and Mrs. Reisling he asked, "Mom and Dad, you want to come?"

"Yes," they answered.

The Reislings, Yancy, and Cecil McGillacuddy climbed into his Rolls. He squealed his tires and they drove off.

Doc Beyer and the other children watched them leave. As everyone was dispersing, Doc turned to the kids who were still there and asked, "Hey, does anyone want to come over to my house and watch the playbacks?"

"Yeah!"

"Cool!"

They climbed onto their bicycles and rode away. Doc could be heard yelling, *"World's Funniest Videos*, here we come! Charge!!"

MOOFLEE IS FREED!

"Sign here."

Mr. Reisling signed the form and the unkempt pound keeper then opened the cage door and Mooflee bounded out. He ran to Erika and licked her face. Erika hugged her big, furry dog.

"Yehh, Mooflee," Michele cheered.

"Cool dog," Yancy raved.

Erika was happy, too, but, suddenly, found herself exhausted by the days events. She looked pale. The world around her began to seem funny. It was as though she was on a pitching and rolling ship and she was becoming seasick. She became faint and then slowly fell on the dirty concrete floor.

"Your daughter!" Cecil McGillacuddy cried.

"Erika!" Yancy hollered.

"Erika! No!" Mrs. Reisling cried.

Erika lay on the concrete floor, her world spinning, her voice quivering. "Dad, what's happening to me?"

"You just did too much for one day, Honey," Mr. Reisling said nervously as he quickly picked up his daughter up from the cold, dank floor. "You'll be all right, Sweetie. You just need some rest. Kathy, help me get her into the car. Mr. McGillacuddy, will you please take us to the hospital?"

"Certainly," Mr. McGillacuddy said, concern in his voice as they all began walking. "What's wrong with her?"

Mrs. Reisling was on the verge of crying. "She's suffering from leukemia and she needs a donor urgently. She's had too much excitement for one day."

"Oh, my! Come on," Cecil McGillacuddy said.

THE HOSPITAL

Later in the day Erika was resting comfortably in a hospital bed. Her mother sat by her side as she slept. There was a knock on the door. Mrs. Reisling answered it and was taken aback. It was Mrs. McGillacuddy. She was carrying a large arrangement of roses from her garden.

"Yes? What do you want?" Mrs. Reisling asked coldly.

"Cecil told me about Erika," Mrs. McGillacuddy said, and then hesitated. "I...I brought these. I'm so sorry."

"You should be. You're a terrible person. You're the worst next-door neighbor imaginable. You took away from my Erika one of the most important things in her life: her dog."

Mrs. McGillacuddy looked down at the floor in discomfort. She hadn't been ashamed of anything she had done in a long, long time. Now she was so ashamed.

"I'm sorry. Cecil told me you did get your dog back. Listen, Mrs. Reisling, I don't expect that to mean a whole lot. And I don't expect yours or anyone else's forgiveness. I am sorry about a lot of things that have happened between us throughout the years. All I can say is I hope to try to right the errors of my ways. I know that probably doesn't mean much, either, but what might mean something is this: what can I do to help?"

Both women looked at each other with genuine surprise. Erika's mom was surprised that Mrs. McGillacuddy's would make such an offer. Mrs. McGillacuddy was surprised at herself. She had found the courage to express her desire to help.

Everything was spinning around Erika as she slept. Blurred and unrecognizable. Sounds were muffled. When the world stopped spinning, she found herself back at Camp Good Days. She was standing over the empty chess table and staring out at the tranquil lake. There were no boats, no swimmers, and no waves. She looked behind her. The camp and the playing fields were empty. Closed up for the season. She glanced from building to building, from cabin to cabin. She found no one. She was all alone. All there was was a relaxed stillness; a silence in the air. But more than that, there was peace.

Erika wondered if she had died.

She turned to face the tranquil lake again. That's when she noticed there were circular waves forming only a short distance from the shore; about in the same spot where they had pulled the prank on counselor Patrick. The waves increased in size and then, suddenly, rising from the center of the waves was Luc. He stood in the center of the waves - water up to his waist - and motioned to her. He was motioning to her to come into the lake with him.

107

"Come, Erika. You can come now," he said.

She began to walk toward him, but then stopped. "I don't want to, Luc," she said.

"It's okay. You can come with me now," he repeated.

"No, I can't," she said, shaking her head. "No. Not now. No."

With that, Luc began to fade away.

"No. Not now," she said. "No. Not now."

"It's all right, Erika. I'm here," a voice said.

She recognized the voice. It wasn't Luc's.

Erika woke up in a bed in a strange room. Her mother was sitting on the bed beside her.

"I'm here, Erika," her mother said to her.

"What happened?"

"You did too much and fainted. We brought you here to the hospital."

Erika then noticed the flowers in a vase on the nightstand. "What pretty roses."

"Doctor Mervis said it's time for the stem cell transplant."

Erika nodded. She knew it was going to happen sooner or later. "What about the donor? I don't have a donor."

"Oh, yes. You do."

"You found one?"

Mrs. Reisling nodded. She said, "Mrs. McGillacuddy."

"Mrs. McGillacuddy?? She's my type?"

"Yes. She is. Imagine that? She's here in the hospital right now, preparing to give stem cells. She brought the roses from her garden."

"I don't believe it," Erika said. "What happened to her? Did she get hit in the head with a brick instead of a Twinkie? Why is she doing this?"

"She's either crazy or she's come to her senses. I think she's come to her senses," Mrs. Reisling answered.

"And all of this time, a person with a matching tissue type was just next door."

In another section of the hospital Mrs. McGillacuddy was dressed in a blue hospital gown and was lying in bed. Cecil was with her as Doctor Mervis and his nurse prepared her for the stem cell donation.

"It doesn't *look* pleasant, Cecil," Mrs. McGillacuddy said with concern as she eyed the needle in Doctor Mervis's hand.

"You won't feel a thing, Mrs. McGillacuddy," Doctor Mervis said. "As I told you before, we're going to put you to sleep while we do this. All we're going to do is insert this little needle into your pelvic bone and suction out some of your stem cells."

"It doesn't *sound* pleasant, Doctor. And that needle doesn't look so 'little'."

"All you'll feel is a little soreness for a few days after the procedure is over," Doctor Mervis reassured her.

"You'll be fine, Mildred," Cecil reassured his wife.

"This is a good thing you're doing, Mrs. McGillacuddy," Doctor Mervis said.

Mrs. McGillacuddy frowned. She was beginning to wonder how painful the procedure was going to be and was nervous. "Let's get it over with before I change my mind, Doctor," she said.

Doctor Mervis nodded to the anesthesiologist who then administered the anesthesia. In less than a minute, Mrs. McGillacuddy was in never-never land.

The straw-like needle went into her hip and the suction process began. The clear, plastic transfusion bag began to fill with the blood which contained the precious stem cells.

Mrs. McGillacuddy never felt a thing.

The first part of Erika's treatment consisted of the conditioning phase. First, they gave her several days of intense chemotherapy. She watched as they connected the small plastic tube to the I.V. bag which contained the drugs that would kill the bad cells in her blood. The other end of the tube was plugged into the catheter in her upper chest. A valve was opened and she watched as the liquid flowed into her system. Erika was accustomed to this part due to her weekly visits to Doctor Mervis's office; however, she wasn't used to having chemo every day and it made her very sick and she threw up a lot. Mr. and Mrs. Reisling were very saddened by the treatment and watched helplessly as their daughter went through it with great bravery.

After the chemo phase came several days of intense radiation. Erika had not been through any of this stuff before and it made her nervous, at first. Still sick from the many days of chemo, they took her into a large room which contained the huge radiation machine, two television cameras, and a single entry door which was six inches thick. She looked up at the big machine. It was as tall as the ceiling and as wide as a refrigerator. Protruding from the top of it was a large, three-foot long arm. The big arm reached out over an examination table. At its end was what looked like a two-foot diameter ray gun from a sci-fi movie; although, she thought, if it were taken down and flipped over, it could have served as a Christmas tree stand.

Erika was asked by Nurse Bright to lay on the examination table just beneath the "ray gun." Doctor Mervis had reassured her that there was nothing to be afraid of from the big machine - that it was going to help her - so she lay down with little concern. As big as the machine was, it did not look threatening. It had been colorfully painted with balloons and joyous clowns. The big arm even had racing stripes stenciled on it. Erika thought the whole thing looked like some kind of clunky attempt at an arcade ride that had been rejected from a Chuckie Cheese's pizza parlor.

"Are you all right?" Nurse Bright asked.

"Yes. No problem," Erika said.

"Erika, I'll be outside. Just look into the TV cameras and talk to us whenever you want," Mrs. Riesling said, pointing to the two cameras mounted on the ceiling. "We'll be watching you."

Mr. and Mrs. Reisling and the others left the room. Erika heard the six-inch lead door resonate as it closed behind them. She was now alone with the big machine, but she wasn't scared. Doctor Mervis had told her she would be in the room all alone and that the others could not stay due to the prolonged level of radiation.

"Okay, Erika, we're going to begin," said a voice over the loudspeaker. It was one of the radiation technicians.

A moment later, she heard her mom over the loudspeaker.

"Are you all right, Honey?" Mrs. Reisling asked, concern in her voice.

Thinking of how Jodie Foster's character Ellie in the movie *Contact* must have felt after being closed up in her interstellar pod, Erika responded dryly, "I'm okay to go."

"Please don't move," said the technician.

"Everything will be okay, Sweetie," Mr. Reisling said with encouragement.

Erika then heard the machine making a buzzing sound. Her thoughts suddenly shifted to her sci-fi camp friend Marvin. She looked at the machine towering over her and nervously whispered, "'Klatu berada nickto.'"

The treatments continued twice a day, twenty minutes each time, for four days, spraying her entire body with radiation.

As the treatments progressed, Erika's condition worsened. She was sick, had headaches, and threw up several times a day. In order for the stem cell transplant to work, the doctors had to virtually destroy her immune system so that the bad blood cells would be killed and that Mrs. McGillacuddy's donated cells would not be rejected.

Every day her friends sat outside the hospital waiting for word on Erika's condition. They were not allowed to visit her because her immune system was being so badly damaged. The doctors were afraid that someone might bring in some cold germs and her body would not be able to successfully fight them off. Something as simple as a cold could place Erika's life at great risk. All that any of her friends and Michele could do was ask Mr. and Mrs. Reisling how it was going.

After the many, many days of chemotherapy and radiation treatments, it was time for Erika to receive Mrs. McGillacuddy's stem cells. The doctors hoped that all of the bad cells in her system were now dead. They thought that *now* was the perfect time to introduce the new cells.

Erika was very weak and very sad. She was tiring of being sick.

"Don't worry," Nurse Bright said one day with encouragement as she connected the I.V. line to Erika's catheter. "There's a good chance you'll do fine."

"You don't know what it's like," Erika grumbled.

"Oh, but I do," Nurse Bright replied. "I had leukemia when I was younger. I survived. That's what made me want to become a nurse."

The I.V. began and Erika was watched closely as Mrs. McGillacuddy's stem cells flowed into her body. The infusion took several hours.

The fear of host versus graft disease was on everyone's minds. This sometimes occurred when the body rejected the new, yet foreign stem cells. It would be weeks before anyone would know if the transplant worked.

During the days that followed, Erika found herself having a series of dreamlike states where she was with Luc on the lake at Camp Good Days.

"You'll be fine," he'd say to her. "Take care and have fun."

Erika said, "Luc, don't go. Let me go with you. I am so tired of being sick."

"No. You don't want to go," he said, shaking his head. "You stay here. You belong here. Au revoir, Erika."

After that, she never dreamt of Luc again.

Several weeks later Erika woke one sunny morning and found her mother sitting in the chair beside her bed, just as she did almost every day since her daughter had entered the hospital. Her mother had good news.

She said, "You're safe now, Erika. No more headaches, no more bad dreams. No more leukemia."

Erika was euphoric. "What happened? It's working?"

Her mother nodded, tears in her eyes. "Yes...yes. The transplant is working. Your fever is down. Your cancer's in remission. Doctor Mervis thinks it's for good this time."

Erika hugged her mother. She said, "I knew Mrs. McGillacuddy wasn't all bad."

"Rest now, Sweetie. Rest. You'll be going home soon."

HOMECOMING

On the way home from the hospital Erika learned from her parents about the remarkable generosity displayed by Mildred McGillacuddy. Not only had she donated her stem cells to save Erika, but she had paid for her entire treatment. In addition to that, she had written a public apology for her conduct over the years towards her neighbors in a letter to the editor. In the same letter she also announced that she was forming a foundation for treating sick children with cancers. She was calling it the "Mooflee Foundation" and encouraged everyone to contribute. She even began lobbying Congress through Senator Clydesdale to have a checkbox placed on everyone's income tax return which would allow Americans to donate a small part of their tax money toward cancer research. Senator Clydesdale had finally gotten the tomato out of his left ear and, with her newfound interest in children's cancer research, had forgiven Mrs. McGillacuddy for her cruelty towards children and animals. He praised her for her efforts and vowed to help her in her newly declared war on cancer.

The car pulled up to the Reisling house and Mooflee was instantly excited when she spied Erika through her hair. She ran to the little girl and plopped her huge paws up on Erika's shoulders. The loveable sheepdog licked Erika's face up and down. She was so happy to see her best friend! Erika, Michele, and their mom and dad all laughed at the dog's excitement.

Mr. and Mrs. McGillacuddy strolled across the Reisling's front lawn and greeted Erika.

"Welcome home, young lady," Cecil said.

"Thank you, Mr. McGillacuddy" Erika said. Looking at Mrs. McGillacuddy, she said, "Thank you, Mrs. McGillacuddy."

"No, child. Thank you. Thank you for helping me see something I haven't seen in a long time. I used to be a little girl, too. The act of caring is what I forgot."

Suddenly, all of Erika friends appeared. Melanie, Jo, Doc, Anna, Peggy, Victoria, Yancy, and counselors Marina, Stency, and Patrick all came out of the front door of the Reisling house and surprised her. Doc held a video camera in his hand and was recording the event.

"It looks like your friends are here," Mrs. McGillacuddy said. "Enjoy yourself, Erika. Come on, Cecil. We have work to do." With that, the McGillacuddys turned around and went home.

Erika smiled and felt really lucky. She was going to make it this time, thanks to Mrs. McGillacuddy. The twinkle and brightness in her blue eyes returned and shined brilliantly, just like the sun over Keuka Lake.

She said to herself, "It was the worst of times, it was the best of times," as her friends surrounded her and welcomed her home.

It was the best of times.

Over the desk in Erika's bedroom, a framed pencil sketch of two children playing at a chess table hung on the wall. In another part of the Finger Lakes, not too far away, at a very, very special place, two chairs beside a chess table were empty once again.

About the Author

Larry Dickens holds an unlimited oceans master's license and is a freelance writer whose nonfiction work has appeared in several maritime publications. In July 2000, he retired from a twenty-four year maritime career where he spent most of his seagoing time aboard LNG supertankers operating in the Orient. He is currently writing children's stories and seagoing adventure novels. He resides in the Finger Lakes region of New York State with his wife, Susan, and two daughters.

Mr. Dickens became interested in the subject of childhood cancers after reading the book *For the Love of Teddi* by Lou Buttino, and the Camp Good Days series of articles written by friend and journalist Jack Jones. In writing *Mrs. McGillacuddy's Garden Party* his goal is to provide an entertaining and fun story that will help people - both young and old - learn more about children and families dealing with life-threatening diseases. As one reader said, "I wish there had been a book like this when my sister was fighting her cancer. I would have understood what she and my parents were going through." Another reader commented, "The book gave me tears and smiles."

Mr. Dickens welcomes your thoughts about this book and can be reached at SuLindHill@aol.com.

ACKNOWLEDGEMENTS

I would like to thank Gary Mervis of Camp Good Days and Special Times, Inc. of Mendon, New York. Since its creation in 1980, his wonderful lakeside camp has helped thousands of young people have fun and enjoy life by providing them with a setting where they can take a vacation from their troubles.

I would, also, like to thank these fine people and organizations in my community who took the time to assist me in learning about childhood cancers, their treatments, and to those who took the time to read and comment on the finished work.

Tod Mervis, Camp Good Days and Special Times, Inc., Mendon, NY
Carla Levant, Social Worker, CSW, of Pediatric Hematology/Oncology, Children's Hospital at Strong Memorial Hospital, Rochester, NY
Carol Vattimo, Parent Advocate, of Pediatric Hematology/Oncology, Children's Hospital at Strong Memorial Hospital, Rochester, NY
The Leukemia & Lymphoma Society of America
The South Bristol Cultural Center, Inc.
Susan Dickens
Lindsey Dickens
Patrick Powell
Cindi Bero, French instructor at Naples High School
John & Jo Ingle
Mary Sherwood
Dr. Susan Sharza
Dr. John Sharza
Jack Jones
Becky Northup
Dr. David Korones
Bill & Jo Kracji
Tom "Stick" & Saundra Farnham
Susanne Kennedy
Bob Anthony
Sarah Yerkovich
Bill & Muriel Coleman

BIBLIOGRAPHY

For the Love of Teddi by Lou Buttino, Gary Mervis, 1983
The Camp Good Days articles written by Jack Jones of the Rochester
Democrat & Chronicle
The Camp Good Days articles written by Ray Hill of the Buffalo News
Gifted Hands: The Ben Carson Story by Ben Carson and Cecil Murphey
(contributor)
In Absence of Angels by Elizabeth Glaser
Blood and Marrow Stem Cell Transplantation by The Leukemia &
Lymphoma Society
A Day in the Life of a Mostly Normal Child by Lea D (The Leukemia &
Lymphoma
Society)

Printed in the United States
4381